The Baal Shem Tov and the Heretic:
A Sabbatean Tale

by

BARAK A. BASSMAN

TELEMACHUS PRESS

This book is a work of fiction. Names, characters, places and incidents are either the product of the author's imagination or are used fictitiously. Any resemblance to actual persons, living or dead, or to actual events or locales is entirely coincidental.

Cover designed by Telemachus Press, LLC

Cover art:
Image of Jakub Frank in public domain

Publishing services by Telemachus Press, LLC
7652 Sawmill Road
Suite 304
Dublin, Ohio 43016
http://www.telemachuspress.com

ISBN: 978-1-956867-52-7 (eBook)
ISBN: 978-1-956867-53-4 (Paperback)

Library of Congress Control Number: 2022950990

Version 2022.12.02

Table of Contents

I. An Unwelcome Guest.. 1

II. The Torments of the Young Kabbalist 6

III. In Praise of the Baal Shem Tov 22

IV. Crossroads 32

V. The Messiah Is Revealed......................................39

VI. Redemption through Sin 46

VII. The Bonfire of the Vanities................................64

VIII. The Joy of an Old Man.....................................72

Other Books by Barak Bassman 75

The Baal Shem Tov and the Heretic:
A Sabbatean Tale

I. An Unwelcome Guest

RABBI ISRAEL BEN Eliezer, the holy Baal Shem Tov, had been feeling uncomfortable that day—he was too cold, then he was too hot; his skin itched here and then there and then in yet another spot; and there was something stale and heavy about the taste of his food. But even though he tried hard to discern why he was so ill at ease—had he accidentally sinned in some way? Was there a threat to the Jewish people brewing somewhere? He could not focus his thoughts and prayers sufficiently to find out the answers to his questions.

Still, he reminded himself, every unpleasant day has an end. Feeling thus reassured, he retired early to his bed, wrapped his blankets tightly around his body, and waited for sleep to carry him away. Perhaps, he mused, everything would be made clear in a dream—maybe Elijah the Prophet, may his merit protect us, would appear to him in a dream to explain the hidden meaning of his irritating day.

But sleep evaded him. He would shut his eyes and they would pop right open again. Rather than relax, he felt his heart race faster, as if something terrible were about to come to pass in that very instant. But what could it be?

Eventually feeling resigned to sleeplessness, he left his bed and went outside to the porch of his fine house in the *shtetl* of Mezhbizh. It was a cool late summer night, and *Rosh Hashanah*—the time when all Israel would be judged—was fast approaching. Maybe, the Baal Shem Tov thought, my soul is ill at ease because I will need to muster all my spiritual strength to ascend to Heaven to plead with the Throne of Glory on behalf of the Jews who had strayed with their many sins. This was always his hardest task: to beg the Holy One, Blessed be He, to be a merciful Father to His children Israel even when they had scorned the commandments of His Torah.

His wife Chana and his scribe, Rabbi Alexander, both followed him out to the veranda and urged him to go back inside and rest. They said they were worried he would catch a chill from the evening air.

But the Baal Shem Tov sighed and shook his head and told them that his body would be fine so long as that was the will of *HaShem*. With the breeze lapping against his face, and the fragrance of ripening apples tickling his nostrils, the Baal Shem Tov finally began to relax. He softly hummed a prayer of thanksgiving to the Holy One, Blessed be He, for creating the beautiful fruit trees and making them blossom so sweetly.

However, his reverie was then interrupted by a man shouting at him in the darkness: Is that you, Rabbi Israel Baal Shem Tov? Standing and swaying, eh? Have you gotten smaller? I remember you as a giant of the Torah, such a mighty saint; but now you look to me like an overgrown cellar rat—are you spreading your little rat droppings about your porch tonight? Does that fine daughter of Israel standing next to you—your Chana, right? Does she clean them up? She is certainly no pretty young bride anymore. Those bony old hands of hers must ache miserably when she bends down to gather the little round pellets going plop-plop from your *tuches*.

The Baal Shem Tov was stunned. No one spoke to him this way—not his most fierce rabbinical opponent, not the most arrogant Polish lord. He was at a loss as to what to do or say in response.

Fortunately, Rabbi Alexander spoke up and told whoever this was to go away, sleep off his drunkenness, and then in the morning beg the Holy One to forgive him for daring to speak such insults to a sage of the Torah. Words like these, spoken in haste, Rabbi Alexander warned, could imperil one's share in the World to Come.

But the man would not desist: I have not tasted a drop of wine or brandy today, he said, although now that you suggest it, my good friend Reb Alexander the Scribe, why don't you send the dried-up crone inside to fetch me something to slake my thirst? And spare me your silly boasts and threats. I am not some fool village Jew impressed by the amulets and parlor tricks of this so-called *tzaddik*. I come to you as an emissary of the true Messiah, who walks amongst us and is bringing forth the Redemption, now, speedily, and in our days, as we stand here and speak. And my Lord Messiah is not pleased with the Baal Shem Tov's lack of faith and his lies. I am here to offer him an opportunity to repent, so that he may preserve *his* dwindling, puny share in the World to Come.

Don't you recognize me? After all, Rabbi Israel Baal Shem Tov is supposed to be blessed with the ability to penetrate into hidden matters, to see into the thoughts and souls of other men. Isn't the Baal Shem Tov said to be like Our Master of Blessed Memory, may his merit protect us, the Holy Ari, Rabbi Isaac Luria, who could read a man's sins on his forehead? So then, *nu*, tell me who I am? What does my forehead say?

But the Baal Shem Tov remained utterly bewildered by this stranger. Maybe he had met this man once before? Maybe he should look at him more closely, with better light?

The Baal Shem Tov asked his Chana to go into the house to fetch a lantern.

She returned to the porch a moment later and handed him the light. He searched around until he could see a tall brawler of a Jew in a large fur hat and an elegant gabardine. He looked hard at the man—there was something familiar about him, but the Baal Shem Tov could not recall who he was, much less see clearly into the root of his soul. There was something hindering his sight, but what could it be? No demon or wandering spirit could withstand his gaze. But this man was somehow impenetrable.

With the light now shining brightly upon his smugly grinning face, the impudent visitor continued: You truly don't know me? Your powers are waning. You are a feeble old man. You belong to the world of lies and illusions that my Lord Messiah is now destroying, and I see plainly that his gathering strength entails your growing weakness.

Let me ease your suffering a bit: My name is Yankel, son of Menachem HaKohen, from the *shtetl* of V. I was once your disciple; I sat at your feet in this very house. I watched you in the ecstasy of your prayers. I too tried to pray with such intense devotion, to elevate all my thoughts, even the impure ones, so that I could achieve unity, *devekut*, with the Holy One, Blessed be He. But I have since gained the wisdom to see through your tricks. I come to you now, not as a disciple, or a pilgrim, or even as a friend wishing to exchange a few words of Torah. No, I come to you now as the Messiah's accusing angel to demand that you confess your many sins and to give you a last opportunity to repent of your wickedness. We must speak alone—and soon.

In response to these arrogant words, Rabbi Alexander exploded with rage, denouncing this Reb Yankel as a sinful disgrace, a latter-day *Korach* defying the righteous *Moshe Rabbeinu* of blessed memory, whom the Earth would justly swallow up. Rabbi Alexander ordered him to leave Mezhbizh that instant and never to return.

But Reb Yankel laughed at this stern rebuke: I am under the protection of both my Lord Messiah and his holiness the Lord Bishop Dembowski. It is you who should fear me. And so, tell me, *tzaddik*, when shall we speak?

The Baal Shem Tov, much to his surprise, felt no anger. Instead, he was curious—who was this man who was so shameless and wild? He did vaguely recall a Reb Yankel, but the memories were a blur—a quiet face in the back of a pressing crowd, an eager but shy disciple. This Reb Yankel had disappeared from his court a long time ago, a fact which the Baal Shem Tov had barely noticed at the time. But now he wanted to burrow into this Yankel's soul and to unravel what this madness was all about.

And so, the Baal Shem Tov thanked Rabbi Alexander for his zeal, but said he was not afraid of Reb Yankel's idle boasts. He was always willing to speak with a Jew in distress or confusion, as this man obviously was, and so Reb Yankel was invited to return the next morning after prayers to say whatever he had come to say.

II. The Torments of the
Young Kabbalist

WHEN THE BAAL Shem Tov returned home after his prayers the next morning, he found Reb Yankel waiting for him on the veranda, slouched against a wall with the same arrogant glint in his eye. Nevertheless, the Baal Shem Tov reminded himself that this man was still a Jew and a Jew who needed guidance. Do not be tempted to anger, but rather have pity and compassion for a soul so lost and wretched and give him the teaching and kindness he needs to mend his ways.

The Baal Shem Tov invited Reb Yankel to follow him inside the house and into his study, a stuffy room with thick dusty curtains, heaping piles of amulets, and a few stray Kabbalistic manuscripts.

They sat down in chairs facing one another, and Chana closed the door behind them.

The Baal Shem Tov began: Reb Yankel, I did not see you at morning prayers in the *bet midrash*. Did you pray with a different *minyan*?

But Reb Yankel laughed scornfully and said: It is many months since I have prayed with a *minyan* other than the holy company of my Lord Messiah. As your prayers are foul and vile, I would never pollute myself by joining them.

The Baal Shem Tov shook his head sorrowfully. This soul was going to be difficult to repair.

Reb Yankel interjected: You truly still don't remember me?

The Baal Shem Tov sighed and said that it was true: So many Jews had passed through his home, seeking help, seeking wisdom, that now, in his old age, he sometimes struggled to remember them all. After all, the Holy One, Blessed be He, had promised Our Father Abraham that his descendants would be as countless as the stars in the sky and the sand on the shore.

Reb Yankel scoffed and continued: I see that I was right. Your famous sight—that ability to read the secrets of every soul whom you meet—has faded. Then you will have to learn the secrets of my soul the same way that other men, ordinary men, learn such things: by listening to a Jew unburden his heart to you. And I will unburden myself to you, for hearing my tale will open your eyes to the lies that have ensnared you.

The Baal Shem Tov checked his anger at these words, deciding it was best to let the madman have his say before meting out any correction. And so, he gently urged Reb Yankel to tell what he had come to tell.

Nodding gravely, Reb Yankel then continued: I was born in the *shtetl* of V. My father was a proud man, a pillar of his generation. He leased several distilleries from the lord who ruled those lands, and he prospered. For my education, it was only the finest private tutors—my father would not entrust his only son to some greasy, twitching *melamed* in a dark basement *cheder* packed with the screaming brats of ignorant louts. No, my tutors were all distinguished scholars in their own right. And I was a worthy pupil, mastering my lessons with ease. Every Saturday afternoon, after prayers, my father would test me on what I had learned during the week. So impressed was he with my progress that he often invited the other householders in the *shtetl* to come over to hear me quote from memory the teachings of our holy sages of blessed memory.

The other boys envied me, but whenever they tried to mock me or beat me, they were severely punished—no one could lay a finger on the town's precious Talmud prodigy. In those happy childhood days, I basked in the admiration of every Jew around me, and I was sure of my path—I would become a rabbi, maybe even a *dayan*, and I would compose long learned commentaries revealing astounding new insights about our holy Torah. I would be consulted far and wide on the most intricate difficulties of the *Halachah*, and my responses would evoke wonder for their searing brilliance.

But childhood days and boyish dreams do not last forever. Shortly after my *bar mitzvah*, my father decided that I had learned as much as I could from the tutors whom he had hired. And so, off I went to the famous *yeshiva* in the town of P. to truly become a learned and mighty scholar.

Although this was my first journey away from home, I was brimming with confidence. After all, my whole life I had been hailed as a genius. I assumed that this *yeshiva* would be more of the same— some study, some prayer, and a great deal of adulation and applause for my extraordinary achievements.

But that glory did not come to pass. For I had been going down the wrong path in my childish folly, and I was now made to suffer so that *HaShem* could ultimately prepare me to embrace His true Torah and to strive for the Redemption of His people Israel.

In my first week at the *yeshiva*, the headmaster posed a problem in which two holy sages seemed to be making contradictory rulings on the same point of law. The resolution of this difficulty seemed obvious to me. I loudly blurted out my explanation and quoted my proof texts, before awaiting the inevitable swooning over my genius.

But there was no praise for me this time. An older boy quickly demolished my arguments, bringing forth an avalanche of texts that had not occurred to me. Another boy piled on, showing with half a dozen additional proofs how foolish my words were. As a third student was about to offer even further demonstrations of my ignorance, the *rosh* gently said that we would move on—although not before adding that he expected that his new student would be more careful with his words in the future.

But while the others moved on and seemed to forget about this incident, I was devastated. I suddenly realized that I was not the greatest scholarly genius of my generation. Angry that I was no longer an adored and spoiled prodigy, I sulked in a corner. I studied, as was expected of me, and could have answered tolerably well if anyone had cared to test my knowledge. But I could not bring myself to speak up again and risk another humiliation.

The other students looked down on me, as they took my silence as an admission of stupidity. I could feel their contempt crawling on my skin in the way they looked at me, in the way they would snicker at me from afar. I envied the boys who shined in the *yeshiva* and spoke up boldly, and I hated them too—I hated their easy way of pulling dozens of proof texts from out of the air, as if by sorcery.

While I was studying at the *yeshiva*, I stayed with cousins of my mother who happened to live in that town. When I first arrived, they were in awe of me, gave me the best of everything, and begged me to throw a few words—just a few delightful morsels—of Torah their way. But they must have heard that I was not shown much honor in the *yeshiva*, because soon enough they stopped beseeching me for words of Torah. Instead, they started complaining about how I was wasting their money by eating too much food. After all, weren't true scholars supposed to be so wrapped up in their studies and focused on other worlds that they forgot to eat? They pestered me continually to write to my father for more money to pay for my gluttony.

Those letters to my home became the means of my escape. Too embarrassed to admit to my father how I had brought such shame upon myself, I wrote instead that my heart longed for a wife and that I was wasting away from loneliness. I begged him to betroth me to a fine and worthy daughter of Israel.

And my pleas were duly answered. My father agreed to a match with another wealthy merchant, and I was invited, along with my family, to the *shtetl* of L., in White Russia, to meet and wed my bride. Because part of the dowry was my father-in-law's agreement to support me for five years while I continued my studies, I was to move in with new my in-laws.

I happily bid good riddance to the *yeshiva* and to my mother's miserly relations.

My bride was a sickly pale girl, who was so shy that she blushed deeply whenever I looked at her. On our wedding night, as we prepared to share a bed for the first time, she mumbled all sorts of prayers under her breath and buried a pile of amulets under her pillow. Then she shut her eyes tightly and breathed heavily. Her whole flesh was trembling with terror. I had great difficulty doing what I was supposed to do—she seemed so miserable and wretched that I felt guilty of some crime against her, even though I was only doing my duty to help her bear a Jewish child.

Unfortunately, my hesitation only made her tremble more.

Desperate for help, I prayed to Lilith, Queen of the Demons, to rouse my lusts. And in response, she dutifully paraded visions of beautiful, shameless naked women before my eyes, stirring within me the desire to do what a new husband should do.

And that night, my Leah conceived a child.

This was the first time that I was shown that what appears to be impure can actually be holy. I had to descend into the depths of the demonic realm before my flesh could muster the will to obey *HaShem*'s command to be fruitful and multiply. While now I see clearly the truth of the matter, at that time I was not yet ready to understand, and so I felt ashamed the next morning for having sought the aid of an evil spirit.

Still, I put one foot in front of the other and settled into my new life as the pampered son-in-law of a rich man. Per the terms of the dowry, I would not be obligated to earn a living for several more years, but rather my father-in-law would support me as I continued my studies. Thus, each morning after prayers, I strode into the town's *bet midrash*, grabbed hold of a tractate of the *Gemara*, and perhaps a commentary too, sat down on a bench, and studied. Now that I was far away from that wretched *yeshiva*, I was confident that my old love of study would return.

But after a few weeks I was forced to admit to myself that there was something amiss. Although I would study all day and sometimes long into the evenings—and how proud my wife and my in-laws were of me then, the devoted scholar, the *ben Torah*—I felt no joy. It was as if I had been invited to a king's palace for a sumptuous banquet and everyone had sung the praises of the dishes before I entered the castle. But when I sat down to eat, and bit into the delicacies set out before me, every morsel tasted moldy and spoiled. Yet who dares to say that the king's fare is anything but the best? So, I would force a smile and pretend to be savoring the awful food that I shoved down my gullet.

And as I chewed the stale bread of the Talmud each day, trying my best to care about the correct way to make a grain offering in the Temple in Jerusalem, should it somehow ever be rebuilt in our days, I felt myself slipping into the depths of despair. I would dread waking each morning, because it meant another day of enduring this dismal toil while pretending to be enthralled.

As I grew ever more bitter and miserable, I found myself becoming impatient with my wife—every one of her questions, no matter how trivial, felt like a rat biting into my flesh. I would lash out in a rage at her, and tell her that she was stupid, that she was wasting my time, that women were a curse. And she would never fight back, pitiful woman, no, she would just burst into tears and say how sorry she was for upsetting me and how she did not know how to be the helpmeet that I needed. But her tears only fanned the flames of my anger. I would roar back that she was right—she *was* a terrible wife, and she should go away and leave me alone.

Sometimes her father would pull me aside and try to persuade me to be kinder to his daughter. She is a gentle, sweet soul, he would say, and she will soon give birth to your child. Marriage is hard in the beginning, you need to learn to forgive each other, to try to lighten one another's burdens, even in little ways. Did I truly wish to spend my days in a home full of strife and discord?

But his words failed to move me. I would storm off to spend the rest of the day in the *bet midrash*, where at least I would be free from the nattering complaints of others. And when I would finally return home, my wife and in-laws were even more apologetic—they assumed that I had retreated to the *bet midrash* for feverish, intense study of the holy texts, when in fact I would just sit there on the bench, like a sulking child, and think about the many ways that I had been wronged.

But in those solitary hours, I made my first, groping steps toward true wisdom. For I asked myself: Why is my soul in such turmoil? I had everything a man wants: wealth, a young bride, a child on the way, and all the leisure to study the Torah.

And how could the Torah not fill me with joy? I thought that I must be looking at the words of the Torah but failing to grasp their meaning, as if the tastiest fruit were wrapped in a white cloth but I could only perceive the cloth covering and not the sweet food inside.

And so, I redoubled my efforts. I read through every commentary I could find, and then I read all the commentaries on the commentaries. I concentrated with all my strength to resolve every difficulty, no matter how trivial, that any commentator pointed out. But even when I figured out a solution to the problem posed, I still felt just as hollow inside my soul.

My wife gave birth to a little boy, whom we named Yehezkel after my wife's grandfather of blessed memory. The whole town came to the circumcision ceremony to share in our *simcha*. I spent a miserable day being jostled by sweaty hands and bombarded with stupid questions about what is forbidden and what is permitted—what luck, the guests would all say, we were just having a disagreement about whether this chicken is kosher, can you, great scholar, tell us the answer?

After the sun had finally set and the guests had left, I mumbled a curse at my little boy for having been the cause of my suffering that day. He must have heard me, because he burst forth with a tremendous, indignant cry. My wife, whose eyes were already heavy from sleepless nights catering to our son's hunger for the milk from her breasts, stumbled over towards him, sighing with her own bitterness.

I walked away. But I caught something new in my wife's eyes as she watched me go: hate. She no longer felt ashamed for failing to please me, I who could never be satisfied. No, her heart now burned with rage just like mine.

That night I sat in the *bet midrash*, alone in the dim candlelight and pondered what to do. I could not continue to study when I knew my studies were a sham and a farce. I saw a choice before me—of life and death, of blessing and curse. Either I must find a way to fill the cavity in my soul with the true light of the Torah or I must end my life. And then the words of *Moshe Rabbeinu*, may his merit protect us, came to me: Choose life so that you may live.

But how to choose life? Death was easy—steal back into the house once everyone was asleep, grab a knife, and cut my wrists. But life meant finding a new path, a truer path, to understanding the Torah. I was not sure where to turn. Still, I knew that the teacher I needed, whoever he might be, could not be found in that town and its dreary *bet midrash*.

The next morning, I told my wife and my in-laws that I was going away on a journey; that I had lost my way and needed to find a new teacher, someone who could reveal to me a deeper and more profound Torah.

My father-in-law said he understood and hoped I could find the wisdom I was seeking. He handed me a purse full of coins and directed his coachman to take me wherever I wished to go.

My wife's face glowed with joy at my departure.

Thankfully, with the blessing and guidance of the Merciful Holy One, Blessed be He, I have never spoken again to my wife or my in-laws.

I asked the coachman what was the farthest distance he could take me in one day. He named a *shtetl* I had never heard of, but nevertheless I told him to take me there. Once we had arrived and he had dropped me off at the inn, I told him he could return home.

I collapsed that night into a long, black dreamless sleep. After I awoke, prayed, and ate, I went to the *bet midrash*. This town was much larger than my father-in-law's *shtetl* and there were several scholars sitting on the benches, swaying and studying.

I told these scholars that I was in search of a new teacher, one who could reveal the deepest and subtlest mysteries of the Torah. They were not pleased with my words. They warned me that the esoteric, occult truths must be approached cautiously—dabble in them without true understanding and you will fall into error or worse. You look like a strong young man, they said, why don't you go into business? That will take your mind off of your troubles. Work and children soak up restless doubts like a dishrag.

But I would not be deterred. I told them how my soul had been tormented, and that I had resolved not to return to my wife and child until I could find the wisdom that had eluded me.

Then the eldest of the scholars there said to me: If you must go down this path, then you need a wise and pious teacher to guide you. No one here can show you the way. But there is a *baal shem* named Reb Yoel, who once studied the *Kabbalah* in the famed *kloyz* at Brody. He could guide you, if you can persuade him to be your master. Reb Yoel wanders from town to town, writing amulets to heal the sick and to open the wombs of barren women. He sleeps in the forest, or maybe in a barn if there is rain or snow. He fasts from one *Shabbes* to the next, so that he can atone for the many sins committed by his soul in its past incarnations.

Where can I find Reb Yoel? I asked.

Who knows? The old scholar replied. He does not spend the day where he spent the night. Reb Yoel was here in this *shtetl* last month; he wrote an amulet for Chaikl, the cobbler's boy. Go to the cobbler's workshop—this cobbler's name is Itzik—and ask him where you can find the man who wrote the amulet that cured his Chaikl's sickness. Maybe he knows.

And so, I immediately left these scholars and tracked down this cobbler, Itzik. He was squat and sweaty, and I could tell from his crude Yiddish—without even a hint of a Hebrew phrase—that he was an ignoramus, an *am ha'aretz*. But still, he was eager to help—he probably assumed that I, too, had a sick child in need of an amulet and a blessing. He said that Reb Yoel had told him that he, that is, Yoel, traveled in a particular circuit around the towns in the area, so that if anything had gone wrong again with his Chaikl, the cobbler Itzik would have been able to track down the *baal shem* to get a new and more potent cure.

I thanked him profusely and directly set off to journey—on foot this time—amongst the towns in Reb Yoel's circuit, in search of the elusive master. I spent several weeks going from town to town asking for Reb Yoel, but being told each time that, alas, I had just missed him.

But the Holy One, Blessed be He, does not abandon His children Israel, and when I was ready to give up in despair, a wondrous event came to pass. In my travels, I reached a certain town very late one night. I knocked on the door of the inn, but no one answered. I went to the synagogue, but the doors had been barred shut.

I kept walking—for I did not want to suffer the shame of being found asleep in the street the next morning—until I saw a light in the darkness shining from inside the *bet midrash*. When I came closer, I beheld, through a windowpane, a Jew swaying over a text, with *tfillin* wrapped around his forehead and arm, and a radiance glowing from his face that was far brighter than the dim candle on the table next to him. Although he appeared to be neither particularly young nor old, he was so thin and fragile that it seemed as if he were about to float away from our lowly material world.

When I opened the door of the *bet midrash*, he stopped what he was doing and looked up. He spoke to me in a gentle voice: Reb Yankel, I am pleased that we have finally met. Come in, sit with me.

How do you know my name? I asked.

What is so hard to know? He replied. You have been wandering around from town to town asking after me. *Nu*, don't you think I would have heard of you sooner or later?

Are you Reb Yoel the *baal shem*? I asked.

Of course, he replied. What ails your soul so greatly that you have sought me across so many towns? Is it your wife? Your child?

I sat down on a bench opposite Reb Yoel and unburdened my heart to him. I told him how I had lost the light and warmth of the Torah; how I felt that something precious in the holy texts was concealed from me. I spoke of how this frustration had blackened my soul and how I had been advised to seek him out as a master and teacher to reveal the hidden truths that I yearned to uncover.

When I was finished, Reb Yoel told me that I was not the first *yeshiva bochur* who had grown restless with the surface meanings of the Torah and now hungered for a deeper understanding. But such boys, he added, often lacked the will to do what was necessary to break free from the illusions of this false material world and to reach into the higher realms. If I wished to be his disciple, I had to prove that I was worthy.

What must I do? I asked.

He said to me: It is three days until the beginning of Shabbat. For those three days, you will not move from this bench. You will study this text—and he handed me a stack of papers—even though you will not understand it. You will not eat. I will instruct the *shammes* who takes care of this *bet midrash* to give you one glass of water each day, which will be your only sustenance. When the *Shabbes* bride arrives on Friday evening, I will test you. If you satisfy me, we shall share in the Shabbat meal together.

I did what Reb Yoel asked and studied the strange text he gave me. It was not a printed book, but rather a handwritten manuscript. The letters were small, smudged, and often hard to decipher. And its teachings were far beyond my feeble learning at the time. I struggled to follow the thread of the discussion of the Holy One, referred to as the *Ein Sof*, the Infinite, and His emanations and attributes through so many different worlds. My body twisted with pain from hunger and thirst, and I grew stiff from sitting in one place. Although I felt weary, I could not sleep.

When the sun began to set just before the arrival of Shabbat, Reb Yoel returned and tested me. I cannot recall what he asked or how I answered, but he was satisfied with whatever words I spoke and invited me to join him for Shabbat prayers and dinner.

I assumed we were going first to the synagogue and then to the table of some wealthy householder, perhaps someone who had benefitted from the healing powers of Reb Yoel's amulets. But we did nothing of the sort. Instead, we left the town and walked straight into the forest. We dove into the thickets, winding and weaving madly, with the thorns tearing at our flesh as we went. If I had not been so exhausted from lack of food and sleep, I would have been terrified.

By the time we finally reached a clearing, it had become so dark that I could barely follow Reb Yoel's footsteps. Here we found a thatched hut, which appeared to have been long abandoned. Reb Yoel motioned for me to follow him inside.

When we entered, however, I suddenly found myself standing in an enormous, brightly lit synagogue. The benches were filled with tall, handsome men, with glowing faces and white robes. The cantor sang in a voice that was so lovely I fell down to my knees and wept.

Reb Yoel pulled me up by my shoulder and motioned for me to sit next to him on a bench. I started to ask how all this splendor could have been concealed inside a rundown peasant's hut, but he signaled me to be quiet.

After our prayers, we entered an adjoining room where a sumptuous feast had been laid out on a golden table. Again, Reb Yoel forbade me to speak. And while I at last satisfied my terrible hunger, he spoke to the handsome men in the white robes about matters of Torah. I could only follow a tiny part of what was said—my learning was too far beneath theirs—yet their words were so sweet I felt my soul to be ascending.

After Shabbat ended, Reb Yoel explained that we had spent the holiday with the souls of holy sages who had long ago left this world and now studied in the Celestial Academy in the World to Come. Their synagogue, where we had prayed and eaten, was in *Gan Eden*.

I now became Reb Yoel's disciple. He taught me how the Holy One, Blessed be He, had contracted His Infinite Presence in order to make room for the universe to be created; how Adam's sin had broken the precious vessels holding the sparks of His holy light and thus scattered and trapped these sparks in our lowly material world; and how it was our sacred task, through concentrated thoughts of holiness and prayers, to elevate these sparks and restore them to their proper place in the higher worlds—to end their long exile.

Reb Yoel also taught me that all souls have their root in a soul that was contained within the great soul of the Primordial Adam. All our souls, he explained, have been incarnated many times before and stained with the many sins we had committed in these earlier lives, for which we now needed atonement and repair.

He instructed me in the ways of the practical *Kabbalah*. We prepared amulets to heal the sick and to ward off demons. I assisted my master in exorcisms to expel *dybbuks*, evil wandering spirits who had seized possession of the bodies of young Jewish maidens. We even once expelled a throng of demons from a ruined old house.

But even though I was eager to at last learn this wisdom for which my soul had thirsted, I was still failing my master. Reb Yoel taught me that, in order to repair our tainted souls and to elevate the divine sparks trapped in this world of falsity and illusion, the true scholar must concentrate solely on Torah and holiness and focus all his thoughts and prayers with the greatest intensity. To do so, we fasted every day but Shabbat and the other holidays, and we drank only water.

For a time, I was able to follow Reb Yoel's austere practices. But then I started to slide into temptation and sin. It began with sneaking small morsels of food into my mouth when I was supposed to be fasting during the week. I had become so lightheaded and dizzy from hunger that I worried I would make errors in writing out the amulets. I told myself this little sin would ward off the greater sin of failing to write an amulet correctly and thus imperiling the cure for a poor Jew's illness.

But little sins lead the way to greater sins. At night, I started to be haunted by demons. They would come to me in my sleep, in the guise of naked women, with thick black hair that fell softly down to their curving hips. With their brightly painted red lips they would call out to me. Although I would resist them fiercely in my dream, when I would awake, to my shame, I would be covered in a nocturnal emission, which I had to quickly clean and hide from my master, Reb Yoel.

Once we were in a large town. I had just delivered several amulets to a wealthy householder whose children had been afflicted with disease, and in gratitude he had filled my purse with coins. As I was walking back to the *bet midrash* to meet my master, I was accosted by a peasant woman who looked just like the demons from my dreams—the same long black hair, the same painted red lips. She was wearing an immodest, tattered dress. In Polish, she said: Three zlotys and I will make you smile, *zhyd.*

I should have driven her away, but instead I simply stared at her, unable to move, so much did she resemble the phantoms of my nightmares. She cocked her head to the side, took my hand, and led me into an abandoned barn on the outskirts of the town.

There, amidst the flies and the rats, she ran her hands over my flesh, and I sinned.

When it was over and my evil inclination had departed, tears burst from my eyes and I ran away, far from that town, into the woods. Tearing my clothes and skin against branches and thorns as I went, I did not stop to rest until the sun began to sink in the sky and I reached a clearing with an abandoned little church. When rain started to pour down on me, I went inside the chapel for shelter.

There I beheld a statue, an idol, of a pale woman with long black hair, probably the Mary who is holy to the *goyim.* As the wind picked up strength outside, I heard a howling that sounded like the laughter of a sinful woman.

I fell to the stone floor and buried my head in my hands. Never before had I felt so wretched. Here I was, having left my home to study the secrets of the holy *Kabbalah,* and I had succumbed to the filthiest of desires.

I was stained and impure.

I was a liar and a hypocrite and an adulterer.

I could not bear to face my master Reb Yoel. I decided that, in order to cleanse this horrible sin from my soul, I needed to deny myself the pleasures of being a student of a wise scholar and to concentrate solely upon repentance. Thus, I wandered through the forest, fasting and praying, with only dirty spring water to keep my body and soul stitched together. I broke off a sharp, low-hanging branch and repeatedly stabbed and scratched myself with it until I felt the blood flow thick and warm all over my skin. I slept in the mud and loudly begged the worms and maggots to slither upon me and nibble on my flesh.

Yet my *yetzer hara*, my evil inclination, would not leave me in peace. I did not dream of holy and pure things, no matter how hard I tried. But instead, my dreams were filled with visions of that filthy peasant whore, her long black hair, her full red lips, her ample breasts. With each passing day, I felt ever surer of the wretchedness of my soul and cursed the day I was born.

Eventually, I took ill. I shook with chills and fevers, and my teeth chattered. As it became harder for me to keep walking in my weakness and delirium, I eventually sat myself down against the trunk of a broad tree, confident that death would overtake me at any moment. My consciousness faded away, and I fell into a pool of darkness.

III. In Praise of the Baal Shem Tov

BUT I DID not die. To the contrary, and much to my surprise, I woke up beneath a soft blanket in a warm bed in a stranger's house. I asked this householder where I was and how I had come to be sleeping in his bed. He said he was the *arendar*, the lease holder, for the nobleman's rights to collect highway tolls. He had found me lying unconscious near the side of the road, and he could not just leave a Jew on the ground to be a meal for a wolf.

You have risen at an auspicious time, he said. It is Friday afternoon and soon it will be Shabbat. Come with me to the *mikveh*, the bathhouse, and we will prepare for the holiday.

After we had bathed and he had dressed me in suitable clothes, he told me that he prayed in the town's *bet midrash*, where the prayers were led by an extraordinary *baal shem*, a Kabbalist master whose soul would ascend to the highest realms as he worked himself into an ecstasy of love and longing for the Holy One, Blessed be He.

That town was Mezhbizh, where we are sitting now, and that night was the first time I prayed in your *minyan*. And my host was right: Your prayers were beautiful. Your whole face glowed like the sun as your words grew louder and your body trembled. No one dared to speak a profane word in your mighty presence—there was none of the usual gossiping about business among the men spread about the benches. Eventually, your hands reached for the ceiling, your body rocked back and forth as if it were being blown about by gusts of wind from a tremendous storm, and your eyes became entirely white.

Later that night, at dinner, I asked my host about what I had seen. You witnessed, he said, Rabbi Israel ben Eliezer, the holy Baal Shem Tov, perform an ascent of the soul to the Heavenly Court to plead the cause of the Jews before the Throne of Glory and to refute the vicious slanders of the Accusing Angel. If you wish to learn more, he continued, go to the Baal Shem Tov's house for the afternoon meal tomorrow, for that is when he teaches his disciples.

And so, I went to you the next day for the afternoon meal. I stayed in the back of the room, and I doubt you even saw my face. But your words pierced my heart. You spoke of how the Holy One, Blessed be He, is everywhere and in everything—*for no place is without Him.* You taught that fasting and mortifications of the flesh were sinful, because *HaShem*, in His Abundant Goodness and Infinite Love, has created food and drink for us to enjoy, not to spurn. If one eats and drinks with proper concentration upon the holiness, the divine light, that has given life to the nature and abundance around us, then a Jew has drawn closer to the Holy One.

One of your disciples then asked the question that was also weighing on my mind: If such pure concentration is the key to cleaving to the Holy One, Blessed be He, then how we can fight off the distracting or, even worse, the sinful, thoughts that our evil inclination uses to tempt us away from the Torah?

And I will never forget your response, which swept aside so many burdens that had pressed down heavily upon me. Your words, as I recall them, were these: Did I not say: *For no place is without Him?* He is there, in those thoughts too, thoughts that you call distracting or sinful. How can this be, you ask, that there is holiness in sinful thoughts? The sinfulness is merely a husk, a shell, concealing something within that is holy and true. When these thoughts come to you, do not deny them or chase them away, for again *no place is without Him* and He is there too. Rather, you must concentrate upon these erring thoughts, think about them harder, burrow into them deeply and find the holy spark buried there—you must elevate them.

And then you continued with a parable: To what can this be compared? It is as if a king had invited you to a banquet and his servants placed steaming pots on the table, with their lids still on them. Only a fool would think that there is no food being served. Instead, you must lift the lid from the pot and scoop out the delicacies inside. So it is with any thought that arises in your soul, no matter how sinful it may appear at first.

Upon hearing your words, I suddenly understood: I had been seeking the divine light of the Torah and the Holy One, Blessed be He, in the wrong way. As a boy, I had sought these things in being pampered and admired. Then I had sought them out in stale discussions of the Law and the Commandments. And finally, I had turned to fasting and mortifications to try to lift my soul away from this material world.

But if His Holiness was all around me, all of the time, then I did not need to torture my body. I only needed to concentrate upon seeing and loving the wonders of His Creation that surround me everywhere I turn my eyes.

That night, after the end of Shabbat, I sat by myself in the little attic bedroom in the home of my rich host. I closed my eyes and concentrated upon the image of the peasant girl whom I had paid to sin with me. I thought about each part of her body—her hair, her waist, her lips—and the moist, earthy smell of her flesh. And as I concentrated my soul upon these things, I thought: She was beautiful—a beauty that could only have come from a spark of holy divine light. I saw now, buried within her foul exterior, a gift, a bounty, from the Holy One, Blessed be He.

Upon hearing these words from Reb Yankel, the Baal Shem Tov, who had been listening patiently to this tale, burst out in anger:

That is not what I taught! That is not how an impure thought is elevated—you must cleave to *HaShem*, not wallow in disgusting fantasies about *shikse* whores.

But then the Baal Shem Tov immediately regretted his outburst. Getting angry at this man now, without hearing his full tale, would do no good. He reminded himself that this was a sick Jewish soul in need of healing and repair.

And so, the Baal Shem Tov said, after a brief pause: Please continue, Reb Yankel. I am sorry for interrupting you.

Reb Yankel, however, did not appear upset. He merely nodded and then continued: I resolved to stay in Mezhbizh to learn your Torah. I asked my host if I could assist him in his business, so I could afford to stay in this town and study here. He said yes and gave me easy work to do looking after the toll collection on one of the little-used crossroads.

I took every opportunity to hear you expound your teachings. But I had learned from my past errors: I no longer sought out glory or distinction for myself, but rather I chose to remain humble and to let others crowd close to you. As long as I could hear your sweet voice, that was enough.

And in your teachings, I was amazed to learn how little it mattered to be a learned man. For so many years, I had been certain that the only way to truly serve and honor the Holy One, Blessed be He, was to squint at small, printed letters, day and night, while parsing the finest distinctions in the Talmud. I was a worthy Jew when I did this well, and an ignorant, loathsome *am ha'aretz* when I failed.

But I realized my folly when one afternoon, on a beautiful day in the Spring, you told the most wondrous tale. It had happened several years ago, on Yom Kippur, when the Heavenly Court sits in judgment upon all of our souls. You had been praying fervently; your soul had ascended to the Throne of Glory, where you heard the Accusing Angel pitilessly recounting every fault and every failing of every Jew. The Heavenly Host were outraged—to this people alone was given the gift of the Torah, and yet they act with such wickedness? Let them be cut down, the indignant angels cried. Cut them down like the vile generation of the Golden Calf!

You were pleading for mercy before the Heavenly Tribunal, but to no avail. You were sure that a new destruction was going to be decreed, even more horrible than the persecutions of the murderer Chmielnicki, may his name be blotted out.

But then a miracle occurred. In the synagogue in which you were leading prayers at that very moment, there was a poor Jew, a shepherd from the mountains, and his son, a boy of maybe ten years. This boy had grown up wild, like an animal in his father's flock. He did not even know the Hebrew alphabet, much less a single prayer. He spent his days watching sheep, catching fish in the stream with his bare hands, and playing a tiny flute he had carved from a broken tree branch.

Yet even though this boy could understand nothing of what was happening around him in the synagogue, he was so moved by hearing the Hebrew words chanted in prayer, and so filled with love for *HaShem*, that he jumped up from his seat and started madly, frantically, playing his little flute (which had been in his pocket). He danced and played wildly, without realizing what he was doing and where he was.

The learned Jewish householders—men like me and my father and my father-in-law, men who had studied Talmud and who knew what sort of behavior was fitting for the Yom Kippur service—exploded in curses and rage and told the boy he was a disgrace and should sit down and learn to behave himself.

But then *you* stopped your prayers and addressed these arrogant scholars. You explained how close Israel had come to a new decree of suffering and destruction, but that when the sound of the boy's flute, so full of love for the Holy One, Blessed be He, had reached the Heavenly Court, the cruel decree was annulled, and the Jews were again inscribed in the Book of Life for another year.

And then I myself, while studying at your feet, merited witnessing the immense power of a simple Jew's heartfelt love for his Creator. It happened on a Friday, a few weeks after you had told us the tale of the boy and his flute. As the Shabbat holiday began at sunset that evening, rain poured down upon Mezhbizh and thunder crashed and lightning surged. Your eyes were full of fear as you started to lead us in prayer.

But then, suddenly, you stopped your prayers, smiled, and burst into laughter.

And the thunder stopped.

After you resumed your prayers for a while, you stopped again, smiled, and laughed a second time.

This time the lightning stopped.

And when you made *kiddush* over the wine that Friday night, for a third time, you stopped suddenly, smiled, and laughed.

And then the rain stopped.

All of us who were gathered around you that Friday night knew that something extraordinary had occurred, something in the higher realms, but we had no idea what it could have been. Still, we knew better than to bother you with our questions. When the time was right, you would reveal what our eyes could not see.

The next evening, after *Havdalah*, you explained what had happened. All that Friday the Accusing Angel had been storming the Throne of Glory with complaints about the many sins of the Jews down here in this lowly world. You trembled with fear that the Heavenly Court would decree some terrible punishment against us all.

But then you saw something that turned the Accusing Angel's flaming words into cold dry ash. In a faraway town, in White Russia, there lived an elderly tailor and his wife. This tailor had made a good living for many years and always celebrated Shabbat with great devotion—he and his wife would don their best clothes and partake of expensive meat and fine wine in honor of the holiday.

But times had become hard for the tailor. His children had married and moved away, and his fingers had grown stiff and clumsy with old age, causing his customers to take their business to his younger competitors. Soon he slid into poverty and had to cut back on his lavish Shabbat celebrations. And by the time that Friday came around, there was no money for wine or meat; the tailor and his wife would have to make do with just a tiny crust of bread to share between them.

The tailor sat alone in his small shop that day and wept. He called out to Heaven: Master of the Universe, all I wish, in my old age, is to honor and serve You by celebrating Your Shabbat with joy. Why must You, Who created everything around me, shame an old man with this poverty?

And the tailor's prayer flew up like an arrow to the highest Heaven, and it pierced the angels' hearts.

That afternoon the tailor's wife found a box of old clothes lying in a corner. She opened it up and took out a frayed, but still elegant, coat. She recalled how her husband had worn that coat so proudly when he had been a young man and how handsome he had looked then. She drew the coat close to her face, to help her remember those happier times.

And then several gold coins suddenly tumbled out of one of the pockets.

The tailor's wife immediately gathered up the coins, rushed out to the marketplace, and bought wine, fish, goose, *challah* bread, honey cakes, candles, and a spotless new white tablecloth. She dusted off and put on her most beautiful dress—a dress she had long been too ashamed to wear because of her poverty—and waited for her husband.

When the tailor finished his prayers and returned home to see, instead of dust and crumbs, a feast fit for a nobleman and his wife dressed up as lovely as the Sabbath Queen Herself, he leapt for joy, and burst out laughing, and grabbed his wife, and danced with her as if he was a young groom again at his wedding, danced with love for the Holy One, Blessed be He, and His great gift to His children Israel of the holy Shabbat.

And as the tailor danced and laughed, you saw from afar what was happening and you, too, laughed—this was your first laugh.

After he recited *kiddush*, the tailor laughed again and twirled his wife once more. And you also laughed with the tailor—laughed the second time.

And finally, after he had eaten the delicious meal and drank the sweet wine, the tailor danced with abandon for a third time, holding his wife's hands and swearing that she was even more beautiful than Queen Esther.

And for the third time that night, you also laughed.

And you laughed not only for the tailor's happiness, but for all the Jewish people, because that tailor's overflowing love for the Shabbat holiday had caused the Holy One to order the Accusing Angel to be silent and depart from the Divine Presence.

After hearing you tell this tale, I closed my eyes and concentrated upon a silent prayer and felt my soul dissolve into all the holiness around me. That night, I was sure I would spend the rest of my days in Mezhbizh praying with ecstasy and listening to your teachings.

But then something else came to pass, which led me to wander away again. What happened was this: A few weeks later I was sitting in a tavern with a fellow disciple drinking plum brandy. I spoke to him of the extraordinary things I had witnessed in your *minyan*. But my fellow disciple merely laughed. That was nothing, he said. Our master, the Baal Shem Tov, has performed far greater feats. And he proceeded to tell me the following tale:

One afternoon you had locked yourself in your study, all alone, and concentrated with great intensity upon certain special combinations of the letters of the true esoteric names for the Holy One, Blessed be He—hidden names that possess the power to crush mountains into bits of dust. You used the magic of these names to ascend to the higher worlds. Yet this time you were not seeking out the Heavenly Court to plead for mercy on behalf of this or that inconsequential Jew with his troubles and sorrows. No, this time you sought the ultimate mercy for all Israel, an end to the very existence of troubles and sorrows: You sought to compel the Messiah to commence immediately, now and in our days, his task of the redemption of the world.

Wielding the might of those true names of *HaShem*, your soul was able to reach the Palace of the Messiah in the World to Come and to break through its bolted doors of gold and diamonds. Across the marble floors you stormed, past tables piled high with delicacies, past a library holding all the books that shall ever be written, until you found him, the Messiah, sitting alone in his bed, tears streaming down his cheeks.

You asked the Messiah why he wept.

And the Messiah said to you that his ears were filled with the moans of agony and pain from the Jews suffering in their long and pitiless Exile.

Then you challenged him: Why did he just sit there in his celestial palace like a *schlemiel* doing nothing? Why not go down, that very instant, to the world and bring redemption, end the Exile, end the suffering?

But the Messiah replied that it was not yet time.

So, you asked: When will the time come?

And the Messiah answered: When the whole world knows and follows your teachings, then the time will come.

With an aching heart, your soul fell back down again to this lowly realm. For you could not imagine a time when your teachings would ever be followed by the entire world.

This tale weighed heavily upon me. How could I sit there, selfishly delighting in your sweet words, while there was still so much suffering abroad in the world? I longed to share your wisdom with other Jews and to open their eyes as my eyes had been opened. And maybe then, if enough Jews convinced enough other Jews, the Messiah would decide that the time has come to bring salvation.

I decided to start with my own family. I resolved to return to my wife and my in-laws to teach them this wondrous new Torah of Rabbi Israel ben Eliezer, the great and holy Baal Shem Tov of Mezhbizh.

IV. Crossroads

THE NEXT MORNING, I left on foot, following the main road under a wide blue sky and a mild sun. I sang softly to myself as I went, and I smiled at the birds in the trees and the worms in the dirt. I repeated to myself what you had taught me—*For there is no place without Him.* I felt the sparks and the light of the Holy One, Blessed be He, all around me, and joy flowed through my veins.

I was in such ecstasy that I paid no attention to the changing sky above my head, and before I knew it, the day was waning, the clouds were darkening, and rain burst down upon me. Thunder crashed so loudly that my ears shook, and a flash of lightning felled a huge tree just behind me on the road.

I now ran as fast as I could seeking to find some shelter, but with rain pelting my eyes and the dark clouds above, I could barely see. I stumbled forward blindly in what I hoped was a straight line, praying for deliverance.

When the storm finally passed and the moon rose large and bright, I found myself in a wilderness of densely packed trees and bushes, with wolves howling in the distance. I pushed ahead through the thorns and the branches until I reached a clearing. There, I was able to make out a poorly maintained, narrow road cutting through the forest, barely wide enough for a wagon to pass through and overrun with weeds.

On one side of this road, in the middle of the clearing, I spied a house with a porch and a stable, and a sign indicating that it was an inn. My prayers had been answered: I would stay the night there, dry and warm myself, and then depart the next morning.

Still, this inn was practically a ruin. There was only one horse in the stable, a scrawny mare that could barely stand up; its weary eyes looked right through me. There were no lights or sounds coming from inside the building, and, in the clear moonlight, I could see the paint was peeling and the porch stairs were broken. But I reminded myself not to be deceived by appearances—*For there is no place without Him*—and who could say what holiness might be concealed within such a dismal husk?

I carefully mounted the steps and knocked on the door.

But there was no response.

I knocked again, louder this time, and called out in both Yiddish and Polish.

At first, there was again no answer and my heart began to sink, but then I heard steps on a creaking wooden floor. As they grew closer, I felt a sense of relief.

When the door opened, I beheld an old Jew dressed in a faded gabardine. He motioned for me to enter, and I followed him inside. On the ground floor, there was a small tavern where the bare white walls were stained with soot. The old innkeeper served me vodka and pickled herring on black bread.

I asked if he had a wife or children there to help him, but the innkeeper said he lived alone.

Were there other guests staying that night? I asked.

He shook his head no.

I pressed on: Is your heart not heavy being all alone in this place? Don't you wish to live amongst your fellow Jews, to pray with a *minyan* in a synagogue? Perhaps to marry a kind old widow who could warm your bones on cold, rainy nights?

But he sighed and said to me: I spent many years living amongst my fellow Jews, and I encountered nothing but blindness and cruelty. I am grateful to *HaShem* for sending me to this quiet place in the woods to wait patiently for the Angel of Death. But you must be exhausted from wandering about in the storm. Eat your dinner. If you want more, go ahead, take whatever you please—I myself need barely any sustenance these days. When you are done, you will find three rooms upstairs. The one on the right is mine. You have your choice of either of the two on the left. Good night, Reb Traveler.

And then, in the blink of an eye, he vanished. The innkeeper made me uneasy—after all, why would a decent Jew flee from the company of his fellow men? But then I reminded myself that I was lucky to have found food to eat and a roof over my head. And again, I recalled your words: *For there is no place without Him.* Anywhere a Jew can be found, there is a spark of holiness, no matter how deeply buried or cleverly hidden. And this proved to be true, for I was to learn that the innkeeper was a wondrous man.

But to return to my tale. As I had not eaten all day, I devoured my herring and bread, and then scarfed down some more food I found lying about in the kitchen until I was so stuffed I had difficulty standing up again.

Ready now to retire for the night, I went upstairs. As I passed the innkeeper's room, a red light escaped from the cracks in the door and illuminated strange symbols above the doorframe—wolves and snakes, which seemed to be moving about in a rhythmic dance. I heard cries of ecstasy coming from within his room, although they were faint, as if they came from far away.

At that moment, however, I chalked up these wonders to my great fatigue—I assumed that I had started dreaming even before I had a chance to lay my head down upon a pillow. I turned into the bedroom on the far left. Once I had closed the door behind me, I was surrounded again by silence and soot-stained white walls. I lay my body down upon the bed and prayed for the oblivion of sweet sleep.

But when sleep came to me, it was a torment. In my dream that night, I was again lost in the forest and again I found this same inn. But when I crossed the threshold, I beheld something entirely different: The interior was now a palace, a vast hall with a high ceiling, brightly shining chandeliers, and a thick carpet upon the floor.

I was greeted by a woman with long red hair falling about her shoulders and burning red eyes. She was wearing an immodest but expensive dress, like the kind that sinful Polish noblewomen wear.

She asked if I was thirsty.

I replied that I was tired from my journey and quite thirsty.

She disappeared for a moment down a corridor and then returned with a cup of brandy.

I asked her whether there were any other guests there for the night.

Of course, she replied. And she called out to you, Rabbi Israel ben Eliezer, the Baal Shem Tov, to join us. And then you appeared.

I fell at your feet and asked you for a word of Torah.

But you did not answer.

Again, I begged and implored you for just a few words of wisdom, a small balm. I wept desperate, pleading tears onto your feet.

But you remained silent.

Finally, the red-haired woman spoke again: His words cannot help you. His silence is a mercy.

But I replied that you were the greatest *tzaddik* of this generation and that I was traveling to spread the light of your teachings.

Now she laughed. His puny words, she said, are not bold enough to redeem Israel. He can see the truth but he fears it, and so he tells you soothing lies to lull your soul to sleep. Still, if you truly want him to speak, tap his shoulder.

But when I tapped your shoulder in my dream, you fell to the ground and broke into two pieces. When I bent down to help you, I saw that you were hollow on the inside.

I recoiled in terror. The red-haired woman came closer to me and spoke words of comfort. She stroked my cheek, and her lips embraced my lips. Her kiss filled me with pleasure and light, and my soul vaulted upward.

And then, in the height of this ecstasy, I suddenly awoke and found my thigh thickly smeared with a nocturnal emission.

The Baal Shem Tov now interrupted Reb Yankel: That was Lilith, Queen of the Demons, who wished to lead you astray. You must atone for your sin with her and repair the damage she did to your soul. That inn was a lair for demons—a ruin far away from any proper human home—and filled with false visions to corrupt good Jewish souls.

Reb Yankel nodded gravely in agreement and continued: You are right, that was Lilith who came to me in my dream. But I do not need to atone for what I did with the demon queen. For you can perceive only the illusions on the surface of things and not their true, concealed meaning. To sin with Lilith is to draw forth the holiness, the divine light, within her demonic husk.

But I am jumping ahead of my tale. I had not yet learned these truths, and you are not yet ready to understand them.

The Baal Shem Tov felt his heart grow heavy. He had heard other Jews speak this way before—men who had strayed far from the righteous path of the Holy One, Blessed be He, and His beautiful Torah. But he told himself again not to rebuke Reb Yankel, at least for now. So, he remained silent and let Reb Yankel continue his tale.

Reb Yankel then spoke again: I could not get back to sleep. I was tormented by my shame—at that time I still believed that I had committed a terrible sin in my dream and needed to repent. But I was too tired to concentrate properly upon my prayers.

Eventually, I decided to go downstairs to find some brandy or vodka to calm my nerves. When I reached the hallway, I again saw a red light streaming forth from the cracks in the door of the innkeeper's room. I could hear the old man reciting strange words that sounded like Hebrew, although their meaning evaded me.

I stood still and listened for a long time. I wondered if this lonely innkeeper was no ordinary man. Perhaps, I thought, he can explain my dream and soothe the torments of my soul.

And so, I nervously touched his door. It immediately opened, almost of its own accord.

When I went inside, I found him sitting on the floor and staring at a wall painted with strange symbols that looked like wild animals, but not like any wild animals I had ever seen. Although the innkeeper did not turn around, he asked me to sit down in a chair.

Once I was seated, he turned, looked up at me, and spoke in a firm voice: You are bewildered by your dream. You have merited the gift of a holy revelation, but you do not understand it. This is often the way with true prophecy. When the Prophet Ezekiel, may his memory be a blessing, first saw the fiery chariot in the heavens, he too did not comprehend. But I can guide you, if your ears will listen.

How do you know about my dream? I asked. Can you show me the way to atone for my sin with the demon woman?

The old innkeeper sighed. And then he spoke again: As I said, you saw but you did not understand. What you think of as impure, is pure. What you call sin, is holy. And what you call holy, is sin.

I told him that his words confused me. How could what I did in my dream—embracing a demon woman, having a nocturnal emission—have been anything but the most wretched sin? And the fact that I saw my master and teacher, the holy Baal Shem Tov, collapse into hollow pieces in my dream was irrefutable proof that I had fallen into the realm of evil and lost the protection of the holy *tzaddik.*

But the innkeeper did not hesitate in his response: The reason you saw what you saw in your dream is that the teachings of your master have the appearance of truth but are empty and hollow within. Your Baal Shem Tov likes to tell the story of how he supposedly ascended to the Palace of the Messiah in the World to Come and was told that the Redemption will only come when his teachings are followed by Jews everywhere in the world. And eager fools like you lap up such nonsense.

But the Baal Shem Tov will not bring forth the Redemption. To understand, however, first you must listen. Let me tell you the tale of how I came to grasp the truth, and you will learn too.

V. The Messiah Is Revealed

AND REB YANKEL continued speaking to the Baal Shem
Tov: This is the tale that the old innkeeper told to me. He was born
in a *shtetl* in Podolia, son of a prosperous wine merchant. His father
was a sad man who kept to himself and shunned the company of his
fellow Jews. But sometimes the innkeeper's father would receive
letters that made him radiant with happiness, which he would burn
immediately after reading them. And also, every so often, a stranger
would come to town and disappear with the innkeeper's father into
the woods for at least the night and sometimes for days.

When he was a young man, the innkeeper busied himself
outside of this strange, melancholy home. He became a devoted
scholar, studying all the time, first in *cheder* and then in the town's *bet
midrash*. He assumed that he would devote his days to learning
Talmud and looked forward someday to marrying the modest and
pious daughter of a fine learned Jew.

But then, one night, everything changed for the innkeeper. The
innkeeper's father said that he needed to speak with his son about
important matters and led him deep into the nearby woods. When
they reached a remote clearing, the innkeeper's father pushed away
the piles of wet leaves on the ground, revealing a metal door that

had been hidden underneath them. They opened the door and went down the steps into an underground chamber.

The innkeeper told me that in this room he beheld a light as bright as the midday sun. He saw many handwritten manuscripts on the shelves there and benches and tables for study.

The innkeeper asked his father what this place was.

The innkeeper's father then asked him if he knew of Sabbatai Zevi.

The innkeeper replied that, like every Jew, he knew that Sabbatai Zevi was a fraud and a traitor—the false Messiah who had converted to Islam to save his head from being chopped off by the Sultan of Turkey.

But the innkeeper's father insisted that these were lies, and that Sabbatai Zevi was the true Messiah who had begun the Redemption, which was still unfolding. He told his son that, before the conversion to Islam, almost every Jew in the world had acknowledged that Sabbatai Zevi was the Messiah. Rabbi Nathan of Gaza of blessed memory had prophetic visions in which Sabbatai's role as the Messiah was clearly revealed. Countless other Jews were seized in the middle of the street with visions from Heaven proclaiming that Sabbatai Zevi was the Messiah.

In their own *shtetl*, the innkeeper's father said that he had personally witnessed many such prophecies. Everyday Jews, women, children, artisans, laborers, would be going about their business as usual when suddenly they would fall to the ground in a fit, their limbs thrashing madly about, their eyes turning white, thick white pus oozing from the sides of their mouths. Afterwards, when they had recovered, they all said the same thing: They had seen an angel who loudly proclaimed that Sabbatai Zevi was the Messiah anointed by the Holy One, Blessed be He, to deliver Israel from bondage, exile, and affliction.

But then, Sabbatai Zevi had become a Muslim after being brought to trial before the Sultan of Turkey. Jews everywhere now rushed to condemn him, to pretend they had never believed in him, and to persecute his few remaining followers.

Before the conversion to Islam, the innkeeper's father had been a follower of Sabbatai Zevi. He had abandoned all worldly concerns and fasted from one *Shabbos* until the next. He had devoted every waking hour to penitential prayers, confession of his sins to *HaShem*, and the study of texts providing moral instruction—*Duties of the Heart* and the like—to cleanse his soul.

When he learned of Sabbatai's conversion, his heart broke. The innkeeper's father was now certain that Sabbatai had been a fraud all along. There was no Redemption. Exile and suffering would drag on, as they always had. The days of this life would slip away uneventfully, like leaves gently falling from a tree.

Yet something still troubled the innkeeper's father: How could all those prophecies have been lies—so many Jews, in so many towns and cities across the world, were gifted with visions from Heaven proclaiming that Sabbatai Zevi was the Messiah. Could they all have been frauds? And for what purpose?

But the innkeeper's father did not dare to speak about these doubts, even to venture a discreet whisper to a trusted friend—for such was the terrible wrath of the community against any Jew even suspected of still following the ways of Sabbatai Zevi.

Eventually, though, the innkeeper's father began to hear rumors of secret groups of believers, including that Sabbatai Zevi still had many followers in Salonica among the Spanish-speaking Jews who dwelled there. The innkeeper's father grew curious about this remnant—how had these Jews kept their faith with Sabbatai Zevi after he had donned the turban and embraced Islam? What secrets had been revealed to them?

And so, he went to Salonica, on the pretext of purchasing wine barrels to resell to Polish nobles. After he arrived, the innkeeper's father went to the shop of a merchant widely rumored to be an adherent of the sect of Sabbatai Zevi. The innkeeper's father shared his doubts with this merchant in Salonica: He could not fully abandon his faith that Sabbatai Zevi was the Messiah—for how could so many prophecies have been false?—and yet at the same time he could not understand how the Messiah had become a Muslim.

This merchant took pity upon the innkeeper's father and revealed the truth of the matter: Sabbatai Zevi's messianic mission had required him to become a Muslim and an apostate. This was because the Messiah can only bring forth the Redemption once all the holy sparks of divine light scattered at the time of the Creation of this world, and now trapped in the lower, demonic realms, have been freed, uplifted, and restored to the Throne of Glory. Yet where were these sparks trapped? Not amongst Jews—many Jews of blessed memory, by obeying the *mitzvot* of the Torah, had been redeeming such sparks for countless generations.

No, the remaining divine sparks still imprisoned by the forces of evil were buried far away from the holiness and purity of the Jewish people and the Torah. To redeem these remaining sparks would require the Messiah to plunge himself into the places of the Gentiles. And so, the Messiah could not complete his task of Redemption unless he should first leave Judaism and convert to the ways of the Gentiles.

This merchant of Salonica taught that the messiah is like Queen Esther of blessed memory. To rescue Israel from the wicked Haman, she had been forced to abandon her Jewish home and to live as a harlot for a Gentile king of Persia, sharing his bed, eating his impure and filthy foods, and breaking every commandment of Jewish Law. To the righteous Jews of Persia, she must have appeared to be an apostate, a heretic, and a greedy whore. But that was all a clever ruse to beguile the forces of evil, for Esther never forsook her people and became the agent of their salvation when they were on the brink of destruction. And so it was with Sabbatai Zevi: While he appeared to have abandoned his fellow Jews and the Torah, he was secretly working for their salvation, struggling to find and liberate the sparks of holy divine light buried deeply within the places of the Gentiles.

The old innkeeper told me that his father was so moved by these teachings that he became once more a believer in Sabbatai Zevi. His father stayed for many weeks in Salonica, meeting other believers, studying their mysteries, and learning where and how to find the remnants of the faithful hidden throughout Poland.

After the innkeeper's father returned home from Salonica, his heart was heavy, as he could not speak openly of these truths, lest he be persecuted or worse. So, he learned to stifle his words and to live with the burden of silence. He was only joyful when he received a letter or a visit from a fellow believer.

The innkeeper was moved by his father's arguments—for how could so many prophecies and visions revealed to so many ordinary Jews have been lies? But, still, there was something that troubled him. The innkeeper pointed out to his father that Queen Esther had completed her redemptive mission while she was alive. Sabbatai Zevi, however, was dead. What was the use of a dead Messiah?

But his father answered him that death in one incarnation was not the end of the Messiah's mission. Did not the holy Ari, Rabbi Isaac Luria of blessed memory, teach that when a soul does not complete its task in one life, it is returned to this world in a new incarnation to continue its work? So it was with Sabbatai Zevi. His soul would be returned again to this world to continue the task of bringing the Redemption.

The innkeeper's father further explained that the brightly shining, secret underground *bet midrash* in the forest, the place where they were speaking, contained the most precious manuscripts of the believers in Sabbatai Zevi, especially those of Nathan of Gaza and Abraham Cardozo, manuscripts full of esoteric truths. The innkeeper sat down on a bench in that underground library and studied these texts, on that night and on many following nights, and he learned much that was hidden from ordinary eyes. He too became a believer in Sabbatai Zevi and walked with a heavy heart and a silent tongue.

But then time passed, the innkeeper's father died, and his mother arranged a match for him in a faraway town. Distraught that this impending marriage would force him to move away and leave behind the great underground library in the forest, the innkeeper made meticulous copies of the most important manuscripts so that he could continue to study them wherever he went.

The first few years of the marriage were uneventful, and his wife bore him two children. But then a new wickedness arose in the house of Israel. Rabbi Moshe Hagiz, a new Haman, may his name be blotted out, stirred up hatred against the believers in Sabbatai Zevi and urged all the rabbis and all the communities of Poland to hunt down the faithful and uproot them without mercy.

Travelers were now viewed with suspicion as there were rumors that the believers were going from town to town secretly spreading their doctrines. In a *shtetl* that was a day's ride from where the innkeeper then lived with his father-in-law, a certain traveler came to an inn and lay his head down to rest. At midnight, several Jewish householders broke into his room, seized him, and searched his belongings. They discovered manuscripts setting forth the doctrines of the believers in Sabbatai Zevi and copies of many letters among the faithful in Poland.

These letters revealed that the innkeeper was a secret believer in Sabbatai Zevi. Word was sent to his *shtetl* and a search was conducted of his father-in-law's home. There, the persecutors found the manuscripts he had secretly copied and brought with him, and they realized immediately that the accusations against him were true.

They bound the innkeeper with rope and dragged him to the courtyard of the synagogue, where he was condemned as a heretic. The town's rabbi ruled that the innkeeper's marriage had been procured through the concealment of his evil ways and demanded that the innkeeper immediately grant his wife a *get* (divorce), which he did.

After he had signed the bill of divorce, the Jews in the courtyard descended upon him, cursing him, spitting on him, kicking him in the head, kicking him in the stomach, kicking him in the chest, until he lost consciousness.

When he awoke, he found himself lying alone in a forest, covered in dried blood. He stood up and wandered about until he found a road and got his bearings. Then he recalled that there was an old man who leased an inn in that area who was also a believer in Sabbatai Zevi. When he reached the inn, the old man was waiting for him on the porch because he had been told in a dream that a fellow believer would be sent to him to ease his loneliness and lighten his burdens. He lived and studied with the old man until he died, and then took over the leasehold rights to the inn.

And then the innkeeper spoke these words to me at the end of his tale: Now I too have grown old after many years alone in this little inn in this remote forest. But I have remained steadfast in my faith, and I have been duly rewarded: I have merited to live to see the return of the soul of the Lord Messiah to this lowly world. I have been told by other believers that Jacob Frank, who studied with the wise and learned believers in Salonica, is the new incarnation of the soul of Sabbatai Zevi, returned again to this lowly world of evil and deception. He resides now in Lanckorona. Reb Yankel, if you wish to see the truth revealed, you must go to Jacob Frank.

VI. Redemption through Sin

NOW THE BAAL Shem Tov felt compelled to speak up again: Reb Yankel, you must know that the innkeeper whom you met in the forest was a demon. I have seen the wicked soul of Sabbatai Zevi being justly punished in *Gehenna*. I know from the many ascents of my soul to the higher realms that Sabbatai Zevi was not the Messiah. The conjuring and trickery of that innkeeper were illusions. Just consider where you found him—in an abandoned ruin in a forest, far from any village or town, with no other Jews about. He could only have been a demon.

But Reb Yankel responded by smiling and shaking his head, as if his patience was being tested by an especially thick-headed child. The Baal Shem Tov again felt he was being insulted but decided once more to check his wrath. A Jewish soul was at stake here—no matter how sinful or deluded, Reb Yankel was a Jewish soul who could—who must—be brought back to the bosom of the Holy One, Blessed be He, and His wondrous Torah.

Reb Yankel then continued his tale: If I had still been a foolish boy studying Talmud at the *yeshiva*, then, like you, I would surely have concluded that the innkeeper was a demon. But having started down the path of searching out the esoteric truths buried beneath the surface illusions of this material world, I was not so certain.

He had made two arguments in particular that troubled me. The first was that there had been many prophecies and visions from ordinary Jews proclaiming Sabbatai Zevi to be the Messiah. Before I had sat at your feet and learned your teachings, I would have dismissed these visions as demonic tricks and lures. After all, I had always been taught that the time of prophecy was long past. Do you recall the tale of the oven of Akhnai, when Rabbi Eliezer disagreed with all the other holy sages of blessed memory? Despite the miracles that Rabbi Eliezer was able to call down from Heaven as proof that his ruling was the correct one, his opinion was still rejected because the holy sages ruled that the Torah is no longer in Heaven—there is no more prophecy or proof by wonders and signs. And when I was a boy, this was my boyish understanding.

But then I learned your teachings. I never once heard you engage in Talmudic discourse. You are an *am ha'aretz*, an ignoramus. My fingernail has more learning in it than your whole head ever will. You learned your wisdom not from study, but rather because, through intense concentration in prayer, your soul ascends to higher realms and beholds visions of divine wonders. If your visions are true, then why weren't the visions of the many ordinary Jews who were told by angels that Sabbatai Zevi was the Messiah?

The Baal Shem Tov now felt his heart fill to the brim with hatred and bile. He had been born poor, and his family could not afford the tuition fees to give him a proper education in the Talmud. He recalled his youth in the Carpathian Mountains struggling to eke out a living by mining clay and lime with his bare hands. In his mind, he heard again the snickering contempt of his brother-in-law, Rabbi Gershon of Kitov, a truly distinguished scholar. Gershon, who had tried to stop his sister from marrying the Baal Shem Tov, because, in his words, such an ignorant, stupid, and smelly boor was beneath her dignity. Gershon who would gleefully dive into the most abstruse and convoluted discourses, rapidly stringing together obscure and impenetrable quotes from the Talmud and its commentaries, and then ask, with the scorn dripping from his lips, whether the Baal Shem Tov concurred or not in the suggested solution to this or that thorny legal problem. Gershon would smirk as he watched the Baal Shem Tov pitifully try to stammer out some face-saving response.

And now this *apikoros*, this heretic, Reb Yankel, also dared to insult him as an ignoramus? And to compare his holy visions and ascents to the rantings of the deluded idiots who had believed that Sabbatai Zevi, the fraud, the traitor, was the Messiah?

The Baal Shem Tov felt his hand clench into a tight fist, but then checked himself. He thought: This Reb Yankel is deluded, too. A deluded Jew should be pitied, not punished. Find the strength to be kind to this fellow Jew who suffers so miserably in his confusion and error.

And so, the Baal Shem Tov chose to speak to him with gentleness: Reb Yankel, visions from Heaven, such as I see when my soul ascends to the World to Come, are different than the delusions of fools and madmen. Perhaps when your tale concludes, we can pray together, with true *kavannah*, deep concentration, and the Lord of the Universe, in His Infinite Mercy and Love for His Children Israel, will show you how to parse the true from the false. But I understand that before your soul can be healed, I must hear you out—no doctor can cure a patient without first hearing all of his symptoms.

Reb Yankel now shot bolt upright in his chair, and his face flushed red. He thundered back at the Baal Shem Tov: *You* heal *me?* You are the fool who needs to be cleansed of his errors.

But nevertheless, to return to my tale, besides the testimony of so many prophets that Sabbatai Zevi was the Messiah, I was also troubled by the difficulty of the redemption and uplifting of the holy sparks trapped in the most impure places. Perhaps a descent into sin such as a conversion to a Gentile faith was necessary for the Messiah to liberate such deeply buried sparks. After all, there can be no life without a spark from *HaShem*. Thus, if wickedness lives somewhere, there must be holiness imprisoned within it, feeding it with vitality and breath.

I decided to seek out this Jacob Frank, the supposed new incarnation of the soul of Sabbatai Zevi, to learn the truth from his lips.

When I arrived at Lanckorona, I took a room at the local inn. Later that day, I went to the synagogue for evening prayers, hoping to hear someone speak about Reb Jacob. But there was no mention of a Reb Jacob.

Feeling confused, I afterwards told the innkeeper in Lanckorona that I was a merchant who had traveled to town to buy merchandise from a certain Jacob Frank. Did he know where I could find this man?

The innkeeper appeared baffled, but then he recalled that Reb Loeb, whose house was just outside of town, was hosting a foreigner, a Turkish Jew—a man who had come all the way from Salonica, wherever that was. Perhaps that was the man I was seeking?

The next morning, I walked over to Reb Loeb's house and knocked loudly on the door. A big bear of a Jew, stinking from garlic and liquor, answered in time.

I asked to speak with Reb Jacob Frank.

The big Jew did not respond. He looked me up and down and appeared to be weighing how much I could be trusted.

But then a voice called out from inside the house: Reb Loeb, stop being so rude and invite in Reb Yankel. He is my guest.

This voice sounded like no other that I had ever heard. The words were in Yiddish, but this did not sound like a Jew from Poland or Lithuania or even Germany. Nor did it sound like a Pole or a Ukrainian speaking Yiddish.

And I had no idea how he could have known my name, as I had not spoken it.

The big Jew did what the strange voice told him to do. He ushered me inside and brought me to a small back room. Even though it was daytime, this room was dark because all the windows had been covered up.

In the middle of the room was a round table with two candles. And next to that table I saw a man who introduced himself as Jacob Frank. He was short but strong. He had no beard or *peyos* (sidelocks), but only a small band of hair between his upper lip and his nose. And on his head, he wore a bizarre hat, like an upside-down cup made of red cloth—maybe it is the kind of thing they wear in Turkey.

He asked me to sit down and state my business.

I said that I had been told that he, Jacob Frank, was the reincarnation of the soul of Sabbatai Zevi. Was this true? I asked. If so, when will the Redemption come? And how do I reconcile your revelations with the teachings of my master, Rabbi Israel ben Eliezer, the holy Baal Shem Tov of Mezhbizh? Which path was the Lord's, and which way was the darkness?

Reb Jacob leaned forward and stared right into my eyes for a long time. I felt afraid, but I could not move. Eventually, he spoke again. This is what he told me:

My soul descends from the same soul root as Sabbatai Zevi and the many others before him who were chosen to be the Messiah in their generation. They each failed in their mission to bring salvation to the world and to put an end to suffering and despair, but I know why they failed and what must now be done.

Man was created in a world that was perfect. When the Holy One, Blessed be He, breathed life into Adam and allotted him *Gan Eden* as his portion in this world, there were no prohibitions or impurities or laws. And this was the way that we were meant to live. We were meant to be men like Esau, strong, powerful lords roaming over our Earth, taking whatever our bodies desired from the fields and trees and beasts at our command.

But then Adam ate the fruit of the Tree of the Knowledge of Good and Evil. Adam felt ashamed and covered his nakedness. He was expelled from *Gan Eden* and cursed to till the hard, barren land for his food—until the Angel of Death would finally take him away. This is the world of the Torah and the Law: death, shame, poverty. It was only in the fallen world created by Adam's wickedness that there were any prohibitions—that one had to distinguish the permitted from the forbidden, the pure from the impure.

The Messiahs of the many generations past failed to grasp these truths. They cleaved to the Torah and followed the Law more strictly, more devotedly and passionately, than any other Jew. But it is these prohibitions that must be overcome to bring us back to our original happiness in the Garden of Eden. By clinging to the Law they strengthened the demonic forces—the *kelipot*—so that their grip on the world grew ever tighter. And thus, no matter how much each of these Messiahs exerted himself, he could not bring salvation.

Each was like a doctor trying to heal a patient with poisonous herbs—the more such medicine the patient downed, the worse grew the sickness.

Everything that is true and good is concealed beneath shadows and illusions. What appears to be holy to you—all those swaying, trembling Jews striving to obey each and every Torah commandment in the most minute, exacting particulars—is in fact evil. What appears to you to be evil—a heretic feasting on pork on *Yom Kippur* or smoking tobacco on *Shabbat*—is actually righteous, as this so-called heretic is demolishing the wicked laws that sustain the powers of darkness.

Look at me. I am an ignoramus. I know no Talmud. I can barely read any of the Hebrew words in a prayer book. I could not parse for you what is forbidden and what is permitted under the Torah. Nor am I the kind of ignoramus whom your master, your Baal Shem Tov, praises and honors. I do not dance around tables singing and clapping with simple, sweet, pious joy.

I have fought and wrestled with men who tried to cheat me in business. One I even beat with a club until I could piss right into his cracked skull.

I have been to bed with the wives of many men. I have made countless upright and honored daughters of Israel into whores just to satisfy my passing lusts.

I am Esau—Esau reborn—and when my belly growls, I seize hold of my weapons and I hunt fat game for my dinner.

Yet coarse and vile as I am, viler even than Esau, I am the one chosen—I am the anointed one. My grandmother was a great astrologer, and when she cast my horoscope right after my birth, she saw that I had been endowed with the strength to redeem Israel from the forces of darkness.

And yet how could this be? I asked myself. I am ignorant. I am sinful. And I have no desire to repent.

And then the truth was revealed to me: I was chosen *because* I am a boor and *because* I wallow like a filthy pig in what is forbidden. These distinctions, between the permitted and the forbidden, the pure and the impure, *mitzvah* and sin, trap us in a world of darkness. I am free from the chains of the demon Torah and the demon Law, and thus I alone can lead others into the true freedom that had been Adam's at the dawn of time.

I am the serpent that must bite the hind's pregnant belly to force the birth of the new, perfect world, free from shame and death and struggle—to restore to us the world of *Gan Eden*.

Sabbatai Zevi was the first to grasp these truths. He blessed the Lord who permits that which is forbidden, and he ordered his believers to stuff themselves like filthy swine on the fast day of the Ninth of Av. But he could not bring himself fully to scorn and despise the Law. And so, the work of salvation stalled before Sabbatai's cowardice.

Yet the Lord does not forsake His People Israel. He used the Sultan of Turkey as His instrument to push the task of Redemption forward. When Sabbatai Zevi was brought before the Sultan and offered the choice of death or conversion to Islam, this was the Lord at last forcing Sabbatai to abandon the Torah.

Sabbatai Zevi's conversion should have been the moment for all Jews to be freed from their bondage. He had now cast off the yoke of the Torah and the Law. Judaism, Islam, Christianity—these are all husks, illusions; they all seek to divide the world into the permitted and the forbidden and thus they all serve the darkness and snuff out the light.

But Sabbatai Zevi still lacked the courage to smash the Law into oblivion.

Sabbatai Zevi began the Redemption, but he could not complete it.

I am Sabbatai Zevi reborn, and this time I shall complete the Redemption.

You speak to me of your master, Rabbi Israel ben Eliezer, the Baal Shem Tov. I have heard Jews tell of his wonders and miracles. Know that he and I share the same soul root—the soul root of the Messiah. He is not a learned man, just as I am not a learned man. He celebrates the simple faith of simple Jews, because he grasps that knowledge of the Talmud and its intricacies does not lead to happiness and wisdom, but only to shame and confusion.

What has this Baal Shem Tov actually done for the simple Jews whom he professes to love so dearly? He celebrates the faith of the little shepherd boy who jumped up during the *Yom Kippur* service and played his flute with such love for the Lord of the Universe. And what happened to this shepherd boy the next day? He went back to his mountain and his sheep, to eke out a miserable existence with barely enough food and water to stitch his body and soul together. And he was probably eaten by a wolf or froze to death in a winter storm.

I am sure you have also heard the tale of how the Baal Shem Tov laughed three times on a Friday night when he saw a vision from afar of an old, penniless tailor dancing with his wife. The man had found some coins left in an old coat pocket and used the money to celebrate the *Shabbat* with a great feast of food and wine.

But what happened to the tailor the next week? He was just as poor—no, poorer, because rather than use his last few coins to buy some merchandise and try to turn a little profit, he had wasted all his money in one night on wine and candles and goose meat.

These are silly tales for silly children. But if you wish to be a man, you must put away childish things. Reb Yankel, it is time for you to end your childish pursuits and to become a man. Join my company of brothers and sisters, follow me and obey me as your master, and you too can be redeemed. I alone offer the path out of the darkness and into the light, to a new Garden of Eden.

As the Baal Shem Tov listened to this insolent wretch Reb Yankel recount the words spoken to him by that abomination and deceiver Jacob Frank, his pulse started to race and his hands clenched into fists. Finally, unable to contain his fury any longer, the Baal Shem Tov again interrupted Reb Yankel: How could you listen to such lies? Having sat in my house and prayed in my *minyan*, having heard with your own ears what has been revealed to me by the Heavenly Court and the Throne of Glory, how could you have listened to this madman tell you that the Messiah has come to destroy the holy Torah, the greatest and most beautiful gift bestowed by Our Father and Our King upon His Children Israel? And that I would share a soul root with this piece of filth?

However, Reb Yankel remained calm and replied without hesitation: But how can I know whose revelations are true and whose revelations are lies? It was you who taught me that a Jew, through intense concentration in prayer—through true *kavanah*— can merit an ascent of the soul and learn new secrets from the Heavenly Court itself. When I was a boy, I thought the path to wisdom was only through the careful parsing of holy texts and learned commentaries. But you taught me that there are more direct paths to reaching the Holy One, Blessed be He. We, too, can be prophets.

Still, at that time, while I listened to Reb Jacob's words, I shared your doubts. I could not yet conceive how the Messiah, the Redeemer of Israel, could wish to destroy the whole of the Torah and the Law—I too had always understood that the Messiah would be the fulfilment of the Law and that, in the kingdom of the Messiah, the commandments of the Torah would be followed without doubt or hesitation.

These last words spoken by Reb Yankel soothed the wrath of Baal Shem Tov. He slouched back down in his chair and urged Reb Yankel to continue his tale. Perhaps, he mused, this crazy Jew was not completely lost.

Reb Yankel picked up his tale where he had left off: As I said, I did not believe Reb Jacob Frank at first. But then again, how could I know whether he had experienced some true revelation, even if twisted and misconstrued?

Reb Jacob seemed to grasp the direction of my thoughts. He said to me: You have doubts. This is to be expected. You are like a man who has spent his life in a dark cave watching shadows flicker on the wall. Now you have been thrust into the light of the midday sun, and your eyes cannot bear the brightness.

You do not yet have a reason to believe me when I tell you that I, an ignorant boor, a lecher who revels in adultery, know profound truths that contradict what so many eminent scholars have taught you for so long.

You need proof.

Come back to this place, later this evening, just before midnight. And then you will see what you need to see.

And with that, he stood up and walked away. Reb Loeb, the owner of the house, returned and led me back outside.

I spent the rest of the day alone. My thoughts were confused and contradictory. On the one hand, Reb Jacob Frank's claim to be the Messiah, who was commanded to destroy the Torah, was madness; it was contrary to every teaching that every holy sage of blessed memory had ever taught. But at the same time, a question gnawed its way into my soul like a hungry worm biting into an apple: Why had the Redemption not yet come? Countless generations had passed since the Torah was revealed to Our Teacher Moses on Mount Sinai, and Israel has been blessed with many brilliant scholars who have parsed and dissected every tiny corner of the Talmud. Yet even with all this wisdom, and all this striving to truly know the commandments of the Law and follow them perfectly, why were we still suffering in our exile? I had always been taught that this was because of our many sins. But do we Jews truly sin so much?

I wondered if perhaps Reb Jacob was right—perhaps the Law is not our salvation.

But then I would feel ashamed of such thoughts and ask myself why the Holy One, Blessed be He, would have given His people Israel the Torah if it was not a blessing.

In the end, I resolved to go back that night to Reb Loeb's house, in the hope that someone or something would reveal to me whatever the truth might be. And so, when it was close to midnight, I slipped past the snoring innkeeper and onto the quiet, dark streets. There was barely a sliver of a moon in the sky and my lantern flickered in the wind. It was only with great difficulty that I was again able to find my way to Reb Loeb's house.

When I approached the door, Reb Loeb opened it before I even had a chance to knock. He said that I was expected, and that, as it was important that I remain to witness what was going to occur, he was required to bind my feet and my hands. I should have resisted—after all, this man could have been a robber, or worse— but I was so desperate to learn the truth that I meekly submitted to whatever indignity was demanded of me.

Once I was tied up, Reb Loeb placed me down in a corner of a wide room. Then he wrapped a thick cloth around my eyes and stopped up my ears with wax. In my helpless state, I imagined a thousand horrible possibilities, and I silently beseeched the Holy One, Blessed be He, to see me through this ordeal.

But even through the wax, faint sounds still reached my ears. There were voices—many voices—both men and women—but I could not make out what they were saying. At one point they seemed to be singing with great fervor. I felt the floor shake; they must have been stomping their feet.

But then the voices suddenly went silent, and everything was still. I feared that someone would now cut my throat. I tried to wriggle out of my bonds, but it was no use.

Reb Loeb approached me again and removed the blindfold from my eyes and the wax from my ears. However, he tied another cloth around my mouth so that I could not speak. Having apparently completed his task, he walked away.

I looked around. In the room where I was sitting, the windows had been covered with thick dark blankets, but there were many candles spread around the floor casting a bright light. There were twelve men and twelve women dressed in identical white robes. Except for Reb Jacob, the men all appeared to be proper Jews with beards and *peyos* (sidelocks).

But the women—even though they were obviously old enough to be long married, none of them wore a wig like a proper Jewish wife. To the contrary, in front of men who were not their husbands, they shamelessly let their hair fall down over their back and shoulders, like a Polish *shikse*.

There was a *chuppah* (wedding canopy) in the center of the room. Without speaking a word, the most beautiful woman there— a woman with thick black hair that fell to her waist and dark blue eyes—walked under the *chuppah* and disrobed.

I was aghast—how could a daughter of Israel flaunt her nakedness before so many men? Where was her shame? And why was no one covering her up again, to restore her dignity?

But rather than show the slightest bit of modesty, she stood proudly with her back straight and chest pushed forward. The others, except for Reb Jacob Frank, kneeled down before her and gazed up in awe and wonder at her naked flesh.

I told myself I should look away—I *must* look away—but I also could not avert my gaze from her, such was her great beauty. I was paralyzed, but also deeply ashamed.

Reb Jacob then approached her, holding a Torah scroll in his arms. He placed the scroll down on a table next to her, removed the chain with the silver pointer, the *yad*, and placed it around her neck. Then he removed the embroidered mantle and the breast plate from the Torah and wrapped these, too, around her body.

Having adorned her like a holy Torah scroll, Reb Jacob now grabbed this woman with his strong, hairy hands, embraced her, kissed her, and fornicated with her right then and there, both of them still standing up, like two animals in the forest. Following his example, every other man in the room embraced the woman kneeling next to him and mounted her.

This was more than I could bear. I shut my eyes tightly and turned my head away.

For a few moments, I heard only the grunting and thrusting of the sinning Jews around me and smelled the sweat pouring out from their bodies. My stomach twisted with nausea.

But then, suddenly, everything was silent.

And with the silence came a new smell of flowers and spices. So delighted was I with this new smell that my anger and my shame were washed away. And I heard the loveliest singing, as if the Levites from the ancient Temple in Jerusalem had descended again to this world to sing their songs of love and praise for the Holy One, Blessed be He.

I opened my eyes again. The Jews around me were still mounting each other like dogs in heat—and even worse, they appeared to have switched partners. But I now realized that the beautiful songs were the sounds they were making as they fornicated, and the sweet smells were coming from their bodies. For several minutes, I listened, watched, smelled, enthralled and disgusted at the same time.

Then the woman who had been standing under the *chuppah* pushed Reb Jacob Frank away and removed the ornaments of the Torah scroll from her body. Naked once more, she walked towards me, with an intense glare in her dark blue eyes.

In her hand she carried a small leather bag.

When she reached me, she sat down on my lap, and spread her legs around my hips. Her head hovered above mine, and her thick black hair brushed against my cheeks and arms. I was terrified. I wanted to flee, but my bonds held me tight.

She gripped my head with one of her hands, with such force that I could not move. With her other hand, she removed the cloth from around my mouth. Then she retrieved a small phial from her bag, which was filled with a green liquid. She removed the stopper with her thumb, pushed the phial between my trembling lips, and poured the contents into my throat.

The liquid was freezing cold—I had never felt such a bitter chill in my bones.

I wondered if she had poisoned me.

But the cold thawed inside my veins and then I became numb all over, as if I were floating through the air. The walls and ceiling dissolved. I saw the whole company ascend into the night sky, past the moon, and into Paradise—into a garden lit by a pink twilight and filled with marble statues of mighty kings.

As we drifted together through the flower bushes and the pear trees in this garden, the woman, still coiled around my waist, changed—her skin and hair turned green and her eyes became a burning orange.

Yet rather than be frightened, I felt sure that I had never seen such beauty in a woman. I reached out with my lips to embrace her, and she lowered her lips down to kiss me. My clothes evaporated into the air—like water droplets—and in my nakedness, I willingly—joyfully—committed the sin of adultery against my earthly wife.

I then broke apart from the woman and ascended by myself above the garden, higher and higher, until I could dimly perceive the bottom of an enormous throne above me.

I cried out unto this throne: Lord of the Universe, reveal to me who is the teacher who teaches the truth and who is the Redeemer who shall redeem Israel.

And a voice answered back to me: Jacob Frank is the Anointed One, the King Messiah, and his teachings are the words of the Lord.

I drifted back down again into the arms of the green woman. She stroked my cheek, as if I were a little boy again and she was my *mame.*

She asked me if I had seen what I needed to see.

I replied that I had beheld the Throne of Glory and at last been blessed to know the truth.

She gently closed my eyelids, and I drifted into a deep, relaxing slumber.

When I awoke, I was in Reb Loeb's house, lying on the floor in the same large room. All the Jews in white robes were gone. The windows were not covered with blankets anymore, and bright sunlight streamed in. Somewhere nearby a pair of birds were chirping away.

With an effort, I sat up and rubbed the sleep from my eyes.

Reb Jacob Frank walked into the room and sat down on the floor next to me.

Reb Yankel, he said, what did you see?

I replied: I merited beholding the wonders of Paradise and I was even blessed with a glimpse of the Throne of Glory.

And then he asked me: Reb Yankel, did you learn the truth?

At that moment, I looked straight into Reb Jacob's eyes and said: I now know you are the Messiah who has been anointed by the Holy One, Blessed be He, and from your lips flow words of truth. I pledge myself to you, now and forever, and I will follow your teachings.

And ever since then, I have been a member of the holy company of brothers and sisters who walk in the path of the one true Redeemer, the Light of our Exile, may he be blessed and flourish, the King Messiah Jacob Frank.

The Baal Shem Tov felt his heart sink at these words. He thought: This Yankel was seduced by demons and tricked by their illusions, just as it had happened in the days of Sabbatai Zevi, may his name be blotted out, when so many Jews thought they had been blessed with prophetic revelations but were caught in the snares of the Evil One. But still, perhaps Reb Yankel could be brought around to see his folly?

So, the Baal Shem Tov interrupted the tale again: Tell me, Reb Yankel, how do you know that what you saw in this vision truly came from the Holy One, Blessed be He, and His Heavenly Court? After all, cannot demons trick men with illusions and sorcery? And why would the Holy One lead you to Him through such a path of sin and wickedness?

But Yankel did not appear troubled by these questions. He said: How do I know, you ask? Well, how do *you* know when your soul ascends—couldn't you also be tricked by demons? I knew the same way that you do: As my soul ascended, I was filled with a light that could only have emanated from the holiness and purity of the Master of the Universe. I had finally achieved the unity with the Divine Presence—the *devekut*—about which you taught. It was your path, your teaching, which was the flickering candle in the darkness that showed me the way to the King Messiah's palace. You were the lantern and Reb Jacob Frank was the destination.

Trying his best to be gentle with this deluded soul, the Baal Shem Tov answered: Reb Yankel, I have ascended to Paradise many times. I visited the true Messiah in his palace in the World to Come. Neither the Messiah nor any other member of the Heavenly Host ever spoke to me of Jacob Frank. However, when I descended to *Gehenna* to witness the greatest sinners receiving just punishments for their crimes, I beheld Sabbatai Zevi burning in the sulfur pits.

But Reb Yankel then responded in an arrogant tone that made clear he thought the Baal Shem Tov was the deluded one: Reb Israel Baal Shem, you heard the words of the Messiah but you did not understand them. The Messiah said to you that the world will be redeemed when all Jews will follow your teachings. And that is what I did: I followed your teachings—that study of the Talmud is not the way to the Divine Presence, but rather fervent prayer that can join your soul to the sparks of holiness that emanate from the Holy One, Blessed be He, in *devekut*, in oneness and communion. When I was at last blessed to achieve *devekut*, I was gifted with the revelation that Jacob Frank is the Messiah. You are like Moses, the teacher and prophet who showed the way to the Promised Land. But Jacob Frank is like Joshua, the warrior who will lead us into the Promised Land and vanquish the forces of darkness.

The Baal Shem Tov let out a despairing sigh. Reb Yankel, he said, it is you who do not understand. I never taught sin. I have always aided the daughters of Israel when their hearts were heavy with sorrow—I wielded the power of the holy names to open barren wombs, to ease the terrible sufferings of childbirth, to heal their sicknesses and those of their weeping children. I helped abandoned wives find their cruel, wayward husbands so they could secure a divorce. These are my ways and my teachings. I would never shame a Jewish wife the way your so-called Messiah does. Can't you see that such wickedness can never be holy?

But Reb Yankel merely shot back a look full of contempt.

Feeling exhausted, the Baal Shem Tov then asked why Reb Yankel had not remained at the court of his wondrous Redeemer. What was the point of returning to Mezhbizh to browbeat an old man?

Now Reb Yankel spoke again: I am glad you asked that question, for it is the heart of the matter. But in order for me to answer and for you to understand, there is more that you must hear.

VII. The Bonfire of the Vanities

REB YANKEL CONTINUED with his tale: And so, as I was saying, I had joined Reb Jacob Frank's holy company of brothers and sisters. I no longer wished to return to my wife or my in-laws. What for? They could not understand the visions of Paradise that I had seen. They would curse me as an adulterer and a heretic and pelt me with their petty grievances.

Many were the wondrous nights that we, the company of the believers, shared together in Reb Loeb's house. I would dance and sing, I would sin and pray, and my soul would ascend in rapture. I drank more of the strange liquids that Reb Jacob's consort passed around—green, pink, orange—and these potions permitted me to walk in my dreams while I was awake.

I attained what you, Reb Israel Baal Shem, had taught me was the highest spiritual state: I became so absorbed in my prayers and visions that I lost any sense of myself as a being separate from the Holy One, Blessed be He. I annihilated myself in true *devekut* and *kavanah* as I fornicated wildly with each sister in our company, raising a new prayer each time I thrust my naked flesh forward into hers.

But *HaShem* can work in subtle and mysterious ways to bring us closer to His truth. Often what appears on the surface to be ugly and vile is actually beautiful and holy. And so it happened to our company: A calamity befell us which ultimately led to our greatest work of redemption. For while we, the elect few, had been blessed to learn the truth of our King Messiah Jacob Frank, we had been selfish in ignoring the plight of our fellow Jews and letting them plod along in the darkness of the Talmud and the Law. But the Holy One, in His Infinite Love and Mercy, brought events to pass so that we would be compelled to come to the aid of our fellow children of Israel.

Here is what happened: The other Jews in Lanckorona, suspicious of what was going on at night in Reb Loeb's house, arranged for a scrawny, clever boy to spy on us. I am not sure how he saw through the dark blankets covering the windows, but somehow, he was able to witness our holy rites. He ran back to the elders of the town and told how we indulged in fornication and ate *treyf* foods and prayed in bizarre rituals, which he had never seen before.

Based upon this informer's testimony, the elders and the rabbis persuaded the Polish authorities to arrest our holy company. However, they had to release Reb Jacob Frank, because he is a subject of the Sultan of Turkey.

The rest of us, myself included, were brought before a *bet din* (rabbinic court) in Satanow. I stood before three trembling old men, buried beneath the heavy cobwebs of their overgrown beards, who were there to judge us. They read the informer's testimony to me and asked if these accusations were true. After all, they said to me, I was reputed to be a learned man and a former *yeshiva* student. It seemed unimaginable to them that I could commit such vile acts in light of my knowledge of the Talmud.

But I smiled and said, in the loudest voice I could muster, that it was all true, every word, and that their beloved Law was an unholy abomination.

The judges were shocked. They suggested that I was unwell—a terrible brain fever, they speculated. As they said to me: If I was telling the truth and my reason was intact, then how could I have no remorse and no yearning to repent?

But I scoffed at these silly old men. I had been told by the Heavenly Court that Jacob Frank is the King Messiah and that his words are the truth. What did I care about these foolish rabbis?

They next asked me if I followed the teachings of Sabbatai Zevi.

And when I answered yes, without the slightest hesitation, their fury knew no bounds and they had me led away in chains.

Still, my example fortified the resolve of the other members of Reb Jacob's holy company, and they too proudly acknowledged the truth of our King Messiah's teachings.

The outraged *bet din* of Satanow dispatched a report of their findings to the rabbis of Brody. The rabbinic court at Brody, upon receipt of this report, issued a *cherem*, a decree of anathema and excommunication, against all of the followers of the King Messiah Jacob Frank, may his light shine forth and may his soul be blessed.

But the lust for vengeance in the rabbis' bitter hearts was still not sated. They now turned to Bishop Dembowski, a great Polish lord and Christian priest. They presented him with their reports and their decrees and demanded that he order us all to be burned at the stake.

The good Bishop, of course, had no notion of these squabbles amongst the Jews. He visited our holy company in the fortress where we were being held and asked us if these accusations were true and if we were criminals and heretics.

I spoke for our company. I declared that the rabbis persecuted us because we denied the lies, slanders, and errors that are the Talmud. And then a sentence suddenly came to my lips, no doubt placed there by the Divine Presence Herself: We believe, I said, that there are three persons within one God, without division within Him.

I was not entirely sure what these strange words meant, but once I spoke them, Bishop Dembowski instantly became our friend and ally. He said that he also was familiar with the lies and heresies of the Talmud, which he had read about in the writings of Jews who had been baptized into the Church and converted to Christianity. He asked if we would publicly debate with the rabbis and expose the treachery of the Talmud—just as the blessed convert to the Church, Nicholas Donin, had done with the wicked rabbis of his day so many centuries before in the famous disputation of Paris.

We agreed at once.

The Lord Bishop then directed his men to release us from custody and to provide us with fine rooms in one of his castles. Once again, the Holy One, Blessed be He, had showered His blessings upon those who followed in the path of His Anointed One, His Redeemer, the King Messiah Jacob Frank.

Terror now seized hold of the arrogant rabbis. They begged that the debate be canceled. They promised to end their persecutions of our holy company. But Bishop Dembowski would listen to none of their pleas.

The disputation proceeded for eight days before a court of Christian priests whom the Lord Bishop had personally convened. Throughout this debate, I spoke clearly and boldly, as befits a loyal servant tasked with the defense of his master, the King Messiah. The trembling old rabbis who came to defend the Talmud spoke in their thin, squeaky singsong, full of absurd sophistries and flowery obfuscations. But I easily rebutted each one of their specious arguments with a string of damning quotations from the Talmud itself.

And they cowered like frightened little mice before me.

When it was over, the unanimous verdict of the learned priests was in our favor. A heavy fine was levied against the rabbis and their followers, and it was further decreed that the informers who had denounced us be arrested, tied to posts, and whipped until their blood covered their backsides.

But the greatest miracle wrought that day by the Holy One, Blessed be He, was that the Gentile court decreed that the Talmud was to be burnt in the public square. Just as my King Messiah Jacob Frank teaches, the Law was to be destroyed so that a new world without prohibitions and impurities could now be brought forth— these fires would be the birth pangs of the new Messianic age.

I led a detachment of the Bishop's soldiers through the many towns in his domains. In each place, I entered the *bet midrash* and the synagogue and pointed out which books were tractates of the Talmud that had been condemned to the fire. The soldiers would then seize the tomes and take them away.

I also led the Bishop's men into the houses of the wealthy Jews—to those whom I knew could afford their own personal copies of the Talmud, and I made sure those books were seized, too. The rich Jewish householders cried and pleaded for their beloved *Talmudim* and fell to their knees; but I spit in their wrinkled faces and laughed at their wailing.

Some Jews tried to hide their books, but I saw through their childish tricks. I would enter their houses, with the soldiers in tow, and demand the immediate surrender of all copies of tractates of the Talmud. They would say there were none—go ahead and search for yourself, Reb Heretic, Reb Traitor—that is what they called me.

And I would walk through the house and, indeed, there would be no books lying about or sitting on shelves. But then I would order the troops to cut open every pillow and mattress until the concealed volumes fell out on the floor. Or we would break down the walls to reveal hidden compartments. I always found these hidden tomes— guided by the Holy One, Blessed be He, I was an avenging angel come to slay the deceitful, wicked words of the Law.

There was this one old Jew, so frail that the wind would have blown him over, who grabbed the three Talmud tractates that fell out of a hiding place in a cupboard, curled up into a tight ball on the floor, and began reciting the *Shema* prayer over and over again in his thin, rasping voice.

The soldiers asked me what to do.

I told them to kick him and beat him until he let go of the books.

But he is an old man, they said to me, can't we leave him be? It is only three books—will His Holiness the Bishop truly care if three books and one old man are left alone?

I realized at that moment that the Holy One, Blessed be He, was testing my faith, just as He had tested the faith of our Father Abraham by demanding the sacrifice of his son Isaac. Would I have enough faith in the mission and teaching of my King Messiah, Reb Jacob Frank, to sacrifice this old man? Or would I flinch and fail in my resolve?

I told a soldier to hand me his sword. When he hesitated, I reached over and grabbed it from him. Once I had my weapon in hand, I beat the old man with the broad, dull side of the blade. Even though I gave him many bruises up and down his bony flesh, he still would not let go of his three precious books. He squeezed himself into an even tighter little ball and kept moaning out his dreadful prayer.

And then I wavered. I thought: Maybe it was not worth continuing this struggle; maybe this old man's stubbornness was a sign from *HaShem* that these three books were meant to be spared.

But no—I could not let my cowardly doubts stop the sacred work of Redemption. And so, I flipped the sword over to the sharp side, and drove it into his neck, hacking at his flesh, ignoring his wails and screams. I even threw down my sword, fell to my knees, and ripped apart the exposed arteries with my bare hands, bathing my face and my hands in the blood that gushed forth from his wounds.

Eventually the soldiers pulled me away from the old man's dead body. They looked upon me now with horror and awe—the same horror and awe with which the Egyptians must once have looked upon Moses and Aaron after the Lord of Hosts had slaughtered every first-born male in their wicked land.

The books we confiscated—thousands of volumes—were piled up in the square in the city of Kamenitz. One foolish Jew tried to rush in and save them, but the Polish guards quickly knocked him down and cracked his bones. The Lord Bishop read out the sentence of condemnation of the Talmud, first in Latin and then in Polish. When he was done, the hangman threw an enormous torch onto the pile of books. The old tomes burst into an extraordinary flame, a pillar of fire soaring high into the sky, just like the great pillar of fire that led our forefathers as they wandered in the desert towards the Promised Land.

We, the members of the holy company of the King Messiah Jacob Frank, saw with our own eyes that our master's teachings were true: We were entering a new world without the Law, where there will be no sin, where, just as it was in *Gan Eden*, everything that exists is good and holy simply because it is there—nothing will be forbidden, all will be permitted.

But nevertheless, I still saw, in the corner of my eye, Jews cowering in alleyways and pouring out their tears and prayers, writhing on the ground, renting their garments, mortifying their flesh. Watching them, I realized that the Jews are still too deeply bound to their tradition of darkness—that they simply do not yet grasp the necessity of breaking free from the yoke of the Law. And then it struck me: It was your teachings, Rabbi Israel ben Eliezer, holy Baal Shem Tov, which had first shown me that truth was not to be found in the pages of the Talmud, but rather in concentrated, intense prayers leading to visions sent directly from the Heavenly

Court. And when I too was blessed with such visions, I was able to see the truth of the teachings of Reb Jacob Frank and to give myself over, in perfect faith, to his ways.

You are the key that can unlock the closed door of so many Jewish hearts. When your soul ascended to Paradise and you visited the Messiah's palace and he said to you that the Redemption would not come until the whole world followed your Torah, this is the meaning of what your ears heard—that your words show the path away from the Talmud, away from cowering in terror before laws commanding what is permitted and what is forbidden.

I come to you now to seek your atonement for your many errors—for your clinging to the wicked Law that your own teachings undermine and destroy—and to demand that you join me in the holy company of brothers and sisters who serve the true Messiah, Jacob Frank. You are greatly honored among the Jews of Poland; they tell countless tales of your wonders and miracles. Now you must tell them that these are the days of the Redemption and Israel's Redeemer, the Anointed One, is Jacob Frank.

Nu, Reb Israel, Baal Shem Tov, what shall it be?

VIII. The Joy of an Old Man

THROUGHOUT THE LAST portion of Reb Yankel's tale, the Baal Shem Tov's heart had grown heavier and heavier. The scale of these sins—murder, heresy, the burning of the holiest books—had left him numb with shock. He had dealt with sinners before, many sinners, but they were sins he could handle: a miser who refused to give charity; a husband who committed adultery; a petty thief; a boy who smoked on the Sabbath.

But this?

He told himself that he should be angry—not just angry, but bursting with rage, like King David in the heat of battle against the enemies of Israel, calling down curses and vengeance for such horrific, unthinkable crimes.

But instead of fury, he only felt exhaustion. He could not think of what to do or what to say—how can one speak of repentance to a man like this, who has a mind so twisted and depraved that he believes that sin is righteousness, and that righteousness is sin? When he looked into Reb Yankel's eyes, he saw the burning, throbbing fever that the Christian priests have in their eyes when they preach their Easter sermons denouncing the Jews for killing their Christ.

When Reb Yankel at last finished speaking, the Baal Shem Tov silently stood up and parted the curtains of the window in his study. He saw that the day had flown away, and it was now dark outside.

The Baal Shem Tov then thanked Reb Yankel for sharing his tale and gently asked him to leave. I am an old man, he said. I need my rest.

Reb Yankel looked suddenly confused and stood up hesitantly. He seemed baffled and defeated by the Baal Shem Tov's soft words. He started to speak, but then the words evaporated on his lips and he walked out of the room with his head hung down.

Once Yankel was gone, the Baal Shem Tov summoned his scribe Rabbi Alexander and gave instructions never to admit that loathsome man into his presence again. He also told Alexander to see to it that this Yankel did not remain much longer in Mezhbizh.

Rabbi Alexander asked what this Reb Yankel had said. But the Baal Shem Tov merely sighed and said that some words should be buried in the dirt alongside one's discarded hair and fingernails.

After Alexander departed, the Baal Shem Tov went to the kitchen, where he found his wife Chana waiting for him. She smiled at him through her wrinkles and said that it was good that he had finally found some time to spare for his poor neglected wife. He had been holed up with that screaming lunatic all day without any respite—wasn't he hungry by now? Thirsty?

Here, sit down, she said.

And the Baal Shem Tov sat down on a rickety wooden chair next to the kitchen table.

Chana served him a plate of warm kugel and a glass of plum brandy. He had not realized how hungry he was—and how glorious and great was the Holy One, Blessed be He, to create such delicious food to eat and to bless him with such a wife, so kind, so patient, and so good at cooking kugel. He thought: If only every Jew could eat such tasty kugel, who would feel the pain of our long Exile?

After he had finished eating and recited the grace after meals, he turned back to his Chana. He reached out, held her hands, and stared into her gentle brown eyes buried under all those wrinkles in her old face. And the Baal Shem Tov felt full of joy in the silence of his kitchen, with his Chana, in his fine house nestled snuggly in the thick black night.

Other Books by Barak Bassman

Elegy of the Minotaur

Repentance: A Tale of Demons in Old Jewish Poland

King Solomon and Ashmedai: A Wisdom Tale

The Twilight of the Magical Siren: A Tale of Late Antiquity

The Leper Princess and The Court Jew

The Last Confession of Joseph della Reina

The Gifts of the Fairy Melusine

Necromancy of the Demon Maiden: A Gothic Tale of Podolia

The Death of the Wizard Merlin

The Vampire and The Wandering Jew

The Emissary from Mezeritch: A Dark Hasidic Tale

The Beheading Game: An Arthurian Tale

The Holy Sinner: A Gothic Tale of the Baal Shem Tov

The Abduction of Queen Guinevere

The Cruelty of the Fisher King: A Tale of Perceval and the Holy Grail